HOLLY JOLLY HOMICIDE

A CHRISTMAS COZY MYSTERY SERIES

MONA MARPLE

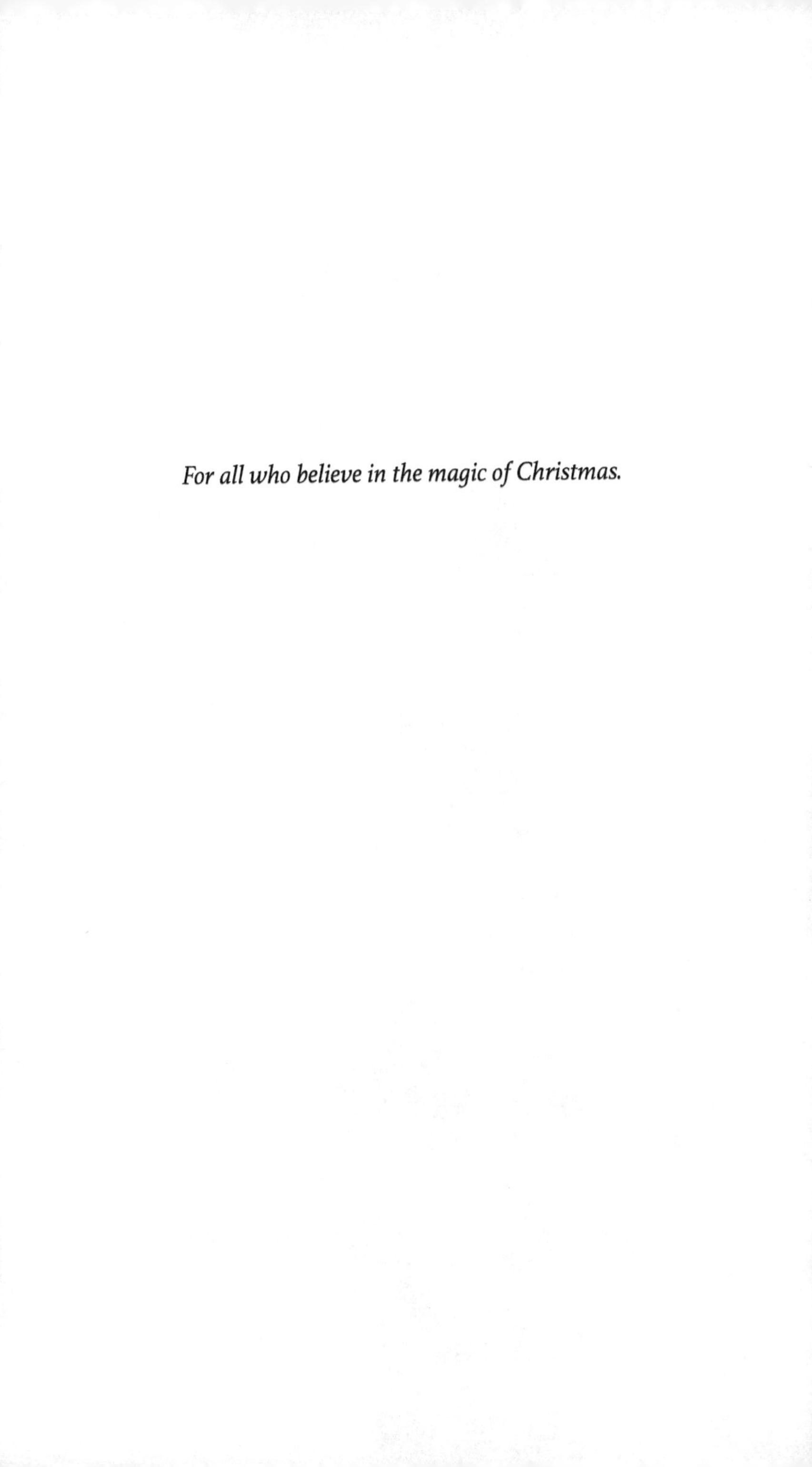

For all who believe in the magic of Christmas.

1

———

Snow fell softly over Candy Cane Hollow, blanketing the town in a sparkling white that shimmered under the warm glow of lanterns and Christmas lights strung between the buildings. The sleigh glided gracefully over the snow, its runners whispering against the frozen ground as a team of reindeer, their coats gleaming under the moonlight, led the way.

"Hold tight back there!" Einstein called out, his youthful voice brimming with excitement. He jostled in his harness, causing the bells around his neck to jingle wildly. "This is going to be the smoothest landing yet, I promise!"

I exchanged a look with Nick, who chuckled and gave Einstein an encouraging nod. "We trust you, Einstein. Just remember what we practised."

Betty, the lead reindeer positioned regally beside Einstein, rolled her eyes and let out a dramatic sigh. The faint scent of her favourite perfume, Chanel No. 5, wafted through the crisp air. "Honestly, if I had a peppermint stick for every time he promised a smooth landing, I'd be rich enough to retire in style," she muttered. "Though I must admit, he's improving."

"Thanks, Betty!" Einstein's ears perked up, and his whole face lit with pride. A moment later, he squinted. "Wait, was that a compliment?"

"Don't push it," Betty quipped, the corners of her mouth twitching into a small smile.

"I'm not sure any amount of money would be enough for you to retire in style," Nick teased her.

She cocked her head to one side before nodding her agreement. "You're right. My tastes do run towards the incredibly expensive side of things."

"You can say that again," I laughed. "I never thought I'd have a reindeer friend with a more extensive perfume collection than my own."

"A woman who doesn't wear perfume has no future," Betty recited, one of her favourite Coco Chanel quotes.

As we approached *The Olde Jolly Hall*, the reindeer began to slow, their hooves kicking up small puffs of snow. The hall stood tall and majestic, wrapped in twinkling lights that outlined its ivy-clad stone walls and arched windows. Warm golden light spilled out into the night, casting a glow that made the scene look like something straight out of a Christmas card.

"This place is perfect," Nick said, his voice warm as he reached for my hand.

I squeezed his hand back, feeling the blend of excitement and nerves that had become my constant companions in the countdown to our wedding. Only six days to go until I married Nick Claus, Santa-in-training, and became Mrs Claus! While I tried to focus on the joy, there was always a nagging worry about things going smoothly. But with Nick by my side, anything felt possible. Even planning a wedding in just six days.

"Attention!" Blitzen's commanding voice snapped me out of my thoughts as the sleigh glided to a stop, the reindeer settling into a perfect formation. "Mission accomplished."

"Perfect landing," Nick praised, patting Blitzen's neck. Blitzen, always the picture of poise, puffed out his chest proudly.

"Did you hear that, Betty?" Einstein whispered loudly. "Perfect!"

Betty tilted her head and gave a gentle flick of her ear. "Yes, yes, Einstein. Now, let's hope Holly's wedding plans go as smoothly as your landing. Let's also hope she reconsiders adding some Tiffany crystal to the gift list." She glanced back at me and fluttered her long eyelashes, and I laughed despite myself.

Nick helped me out of the sleigh, and my boots crunched into the snow as I stepped down. The crisp air nipped at my cheeks, but the sight of *The Olde Jolly Hall* made the chill worth it. This was the place where our forever would begin, steeped in history and holiday magic.

"Welcome, lovebirds!" A friendly voice called to us. I guessed that the woman must be Paula Adams, the member of staff who had agreed to see us at such short notice. Clipboard in hand, she was the embodiment of efficiency, with her neatly pinned hair and a smile that could warm even the frostiest of hearts. "We've got lots to go over."

"You must be Paula?" I asked as Nick and I crossed the lawn and headed towards the hall's entrance.

"Paula Adams, pleased to meet you, Holly. And you, Nick. Follow me."

We walked up the stone steps, the garlands lining the handrails brushing softly against my coat. Inside, the hall was even more breathtaking than it looked in the brochure. The scent of cinnamon and pine wrapped around us as we stepped into the entryway. High wooden beams draped in evergreen garlands crisscrossed above, and wreaths adorned with red velvet ribbons hung at perfect intervals along the walls. At the far end, a grand Christmas tree sparkled, at least twenty feet tall, its branches heavy with ornaments and ribbon that cascaded like a waterfall of gold and crimson.

"This place is even more beautiful than I expected," I murmured, taking in the warm glow of candles flickering in sconces and the gentle hum of a carol playing from somewhere unseen. The room practically pulsed with history, every corner whispering stories of holiday gatherings and joyous celebrations past.

"Right, let's start with the layout for the ceremony," Paula said, her pen poised above her notepad. "You'll walk down the aisle here, past the pews lined with holly and mistletoe, and—"

Her voice faded into the background as I let my eyes wander, soaking in every detail. My gaze landed on a small brass sconce near the far wall, carved with intricate holly leaves. Something about it seemed out of place, almost as if it had a purpose beyond mere decoration.

Instinct nudged me forward. Before I knew it, my fingers brushed the cold brass, and I pressed it gently. A soft click echoed through the hall, and a section of the wooden panelling shifted and creaked open, revealing a narrow, dimly lit passageway.

"Holly?" Nick's voice was sharp, but I turned back to give him a reassuring smile before curiosity propelled me into the hidden corridor.

The air was cool and carried a musty scent, tinged with pine and dust. The narrow hallway curved sharply, leading to a small room lined with old shelves and boxes marked with the Harper family crest. The Harpers had owned the hall for generations. The brochure had explained the history of the building and the family, as if the two were completely intertwined, which I guess they were. An ancient-looking lantern cast a flickering light, throwing long, shadowy fingers across the room.

"Ah!" I cried out, my voice wavering as my eyes locked onto the far corner. There, nestled between a toppled chair and an old trunk, was the motionless figure of a woman. Golden curls, dulled by dust, framed her pale face, and an expensive emerald brooch glinted on her chest.

"Paula! Nick!" I yelled, my breath coming in short, sharp gasps. "I've found something!"

Paula's footsteps echoed through the passage as she hurried to join me. "What is it?" she called, her voice tinged with alarm.

"I... I think it's a woman," I said, swallowing hard. My heart raced, the festive warmth of the hall now replaced with an icy chill. "She's not moving."

The silence that followed was as deep as the winter night outside, heavy with the weight of discovery and the whispered echoes of secrets long kept.

**

The discovery left me trembling. I leaned against the doorframe of the hidden passage, trying to steady my breathing as Paula crouched beside the still figure. Nick hovered just behind me, his steady presence the only thing keeping me from spiralling into panic.

"Oh no," Paula whispered, her voice trembling as she leaned closer. "It's... it's Beatrice."

My breath caught. "Beatrice?" I echoed. "You know her?"

Paula nodded, her face pale as she turned to look at me.

"Beatrice Harper. She owns this hall. I've known her since she was a little girl." Her voice broke slightly, and she pressed a hand to her mouth. "This can't be happening."

Nick placed a steadying hand on Paula's shoulder. "We'll call the police immediately," he said, his voice calm and firm. "But we need to leave this area untouched. It's a crime scene now."

I took a step back, the weight of Paula's words pressing down on me. Beatrice Harper. The name was familiar from the hall's brochure, where her photo had been proudly displayed alongside a history of the Harper family. She'd inherited the hall recently, after her mother's death, the latest in a long line of Harpers to oversee its legacy. And now...

"Nick's right," I managed, my voice shaking. "We should go back to the main hall. Give the police room to work when they arrive."

Paula hesitated, her eyes lingering on Beatrice's lifeless form before she nodded and rose unsteadily to her feet. "I'll call Charles and Melinda," she murmured. "They need to know."

We made our way back into the grand hall, the festive decorations that had charmed me earlier now feeling strangely hollow. Paula disappeared into a side office to make her call, and Nick led me to a seating area near the towering Christmas tree. I sank into a plush chair, still struggling to process what had just happened.

It wasn't long before hurried footsteps echoed across the hall, and two figures emerged from the far doorway. The man was in his late thirties, his dark hair neatly combed and his tailored suit immaculate, save for the loosened tie around his neck. His sharp green eyes flicked over me and Nick briefly, an air of disinterest clouding his expression.

The woman beside him, however, was the picture of composure. Her coat, a deep shade of forest green, was cinched perfectly at the waist, and her heeled boots clicked against the polished floor as she approached. Her gaze swept the room, assessing everything in an instant, before she stopped beside Paula.

"What's going on?" the man asked, his voice clipped. "Paula sounded hysterical. I've told her a hundred times about interruptions when I'm working."

Paula stepped forward, her hands trembling slightly as she gestured towards me and Nick. "Charles, Melinda, this is Holly Wood and Nick Claus. They're planning their wedding here. Holly... she's the one who found her."

"Found who?" Charles pressed, his tone impatient. "I couldn't understand a darn word you said on the phone."

Paula took a shaky breath. "Beatrice. She's... she's gone, Charles."

"Yes, thank you, very good. We know she's gone. She's hardly lost! She's rediscovering herself or some nonsense in Bali. Now can I return to my desk?"

"They found her in one of the old passageways."

For a moment, silence hung heavy in the air. Melinda's polished composure slipped, her eyes widening as her hand flew to her mouth. "Beatrice?" she whispered, her voice trembling. "No... that can't be right."

Charles, on the other hand, gave a short laugh. "She's a lot further away than that, Paula. What's got into you? You know Beatrice is out of the country."

Paula shook her head, tears glistening in her eyes. "It's her, Charles. I'd recognise her anywhere. She's... she's dead."

"This is nonsense," he said.

"Paula wouldn't lie about something like this, Charlie. I don't understand it, either, but if Paula says it, I believe her."

Charles groaned. "You women have always had me outnumbered. Fine, fine, my darling sister who emailed me a sunset photo just last night, is actually dead in a passageway."

I felt a chill run down my spine at his reaction—or rather, his lack of one. "You don't seem very emotional," I said cautiously, my eyes narrowing as I studied him.

Charles turned his gaze to me, his expression unreadable. "Should I be?" he replied coolly. "For a start, I won't believe it until I see it. But, let's suppose it's true for a moment. It would be tragic, of course, but people don't just turn up dead in hidden passageways without a good reason."

"Charles!" Melinda snapped, her tone sharp. "That's your sister you're talking about."

"And I'm acknowledging the reality of the situation," Charles shot back. "If she's dead, then someone's responsible. Wringing our hands won't change that."

Nick stepped forward, his jaw tightening. "You could at least show a little compassion."

Charles shrugged, shoving his hands into his pockets. "Compassion won't bring her back... from her holiday or from the dead."

Melinda let out a shaky breath, her eyes darting between Charles and me. "I'm sorry," she said, her voice softening as she addressed me directly. "Charles isn't... well, he doesn't handle emotions like most people. Please don't take it personally."

I nodded slowly, though unease continued to coil in my stomach. "I understand. But this is a serious matter. The police will be here soon, and they'll have questions for all of us."

"Of course," Melinda replied, her tone crisp once more. "We'll do whatever we can to help. Paula, would you mind showing us the area where... where Beatrice was found?"

Paula hesitated, glancing at me for a moment before nodding. "Of course. I'll take you there now."

As the three of them disappeared into the passageway, Nick leaned closer to me, his voice low. "What do you make of him?"

"Charles?" I whispered back. "I don't know. He's... cold. Too cold. But Melinda seemed genuinely upset."

Nick nodded, his eyes narrowing thoughtfully. "There's something strange about him. We need to keep an eye on that one."

I glanced back at the corridor, where shadows danced faintly against the walls. The festive warmth of the hall seemed to dim, leaving only a heavy, uneasy silence in its wake.

2

———————

I paced near the towering Christmas tree in the main hall, the sound of low voices drifting from near the passageway where Beatrice's body had been found. I couldn't hear what Charles and Paula were discussing, but they both wore grim expressions on their faces. Melinda was engrossed in her phone, tapping away as she leaned against the wall. My hands fiddled with the hem of my coat, though no amount of tugging seemed to settle the buzzing in my mind.

"Any word from Wiggles?" Nick asked, his hand lightly brushing mine in a silent offer of comfort.

I shook my head. "No, not yet. I thought he'd be here by now." I glanced out the frosted window, hoping to see Wiggles' tiny Fiat pulling into the snowy drive, but there was no sign of his arrival.

As if summoned by my thoughts, my phone buzzed in my pocket. I pulled it out, seeing Wiggles' name flash across the screen. Relief flooded through me as I answered. "Wiggles! Where are you?"

His voice, cheerful as ever, practically burst through the

receiver. "Holly, you won't believe this—I'm stuck in a queue for emergency candy cane repairs!"

"Candy cane repairs?" I echoed, blinking. Nick raised an eyebrow, his curiosity piqued.

"Yes! Mrs Claus went all out this year, but half the big display canes outside the workshop snapped in last night's snowstorm. I've got reindeer jingling at me to hurry up, a queue of elves in crisis, and the candy cane glue is frozen solid. It's utter chaos."

Despite myself, I smiled. Wiggles and his festive emergencies were as predictable as snow at Christmas. "I hope you get it sorted soon. We could really use you here."

"I'll be there as soon as I can, promise," he said. "Just... try not to let anything ruin the wedding, okay? I'll bring backup candy canes with me when I can get there!"

The line clicked off before I could respond, and I stared at my phone for a moment before slipping it back into my pocket.

"Well?" Nick prompted.

"He's dealing with a candy cane catastrophe." I rolled my eyes, though a small smile tugged at my lips.

Nick chuckled. "Classic Wiggles. So what now?"

Before I could answer, the sound of the main doors creaking open drew my attention. Gilbert, dressed in his usual impeccable chef's whites beneath a heavy wool coat, strode into the hall, his expression a mix of concern and irritation.

"Well, this is a fine how-do-you-do," he announced, shrugging off his coat and handing it to a bemused Paula, who had instinctively moved towards him as if in greeting. "I'm up to my elbows in wedding canapés, and now I hear there's a murder in the mix. Honestly, Holly, if this is some elaborate ploy to stress me out before the big day, you'll be getting my resignation faster than you can say dead-as-a-dodo!"

I stifled a laugh. "Gilbert, what are you doing here?"

"Wiggles sent me," he replied with a dramatic wave of his hand. "Said he was otherwise occupied saving the world —or candy canes, same difference."

Nick leaned closer to me and muttered, "We're definitely going to need Wiggles' backup canes."

I bit back a grin and focused on Gilbert. "Thanks for coming. It's been... a lot."

Gilbert's sharp eyes softened slightly. "I can imagine. I'm not entirely sure what I've walked into, but if it involves bodies in hidden passageways, you'd best keep me out of it. I don't do well with drama that isn't of my own making."

Nick chuckled, but I couldn't quite summon the same humour. My thoughts turned to Beatrice, to Paula's shaken face, and to Charles' chilling indifference. The festive magic of the hall now felt dulled, overshadowed by questions that clawed at the edges of my mind.

"I just..." I hesitated, glancing at Nick. "What if this ruins everything? What if the wedding can't go ahead because of —well, this?"

Nick's hand tightened around mine. "It won't ruin anything. We'll find a way."

Gilbert clapped his hands together. "Right, then. What's the plan? Surely you're not thinking of cancelling?"

I took a deep breath, my thoughts racing. The police would do their job, of course, but what if they didn't move fast enough? What if Beatrice's death cast such a long shadow over the hall that the idea of a wedding here became unthinkable?

"No one's cancelling anything," I said firmly, my voice

steadier than I felt. "But... maybe there's something I can do to help."

Nick frowned. "You mean investigate?"

"I mean, someone has to make sure this doesn't put the wedding at risk." I paused, scanning his face for a reaction. "If Wiggles were here, he'd be saying the same thing."

"Wiggles would also insist on a safety helmet and a chocolate break every twenty minutes," Nick said, though his tone was more thoughtful than dismissive.

Gilbert crossed his arms. "As long as this doesn't involve me crawling through passageways or getting blood on my whites, I'm happy to lend my expertise. And by expertise, I mean standing here looking decorative while you do all the work."

A small laugh escaped me despite the weight in my chest. "Noted, Gilbert. Thanks."

As the three of us stood beneath the Christmas tree, I couldn't help but feel the first stirrings of determination. Beatrice's death was a tragedy, but I wouldn't let it derail everything Nick and I had worked towards. Somehow, we'd find answers—and we'd make it to our wedding day.

**

The makeshift cordon didn't look particularly official, but it would have to do. Nick and I had tied together a couple of festive red-and-white ribbons from the tree decorations to block the entrance to the passageway where Beatrice's body had been discovered. I had no illusions that it would deter anyone particularly determined, but for now, it was enough to make the area feel off-limits.

Gilbert eyed our handiwork with a sceptical raise of his brow. "*Very* professional. I'm sure this will keep out the nosiest of intruders."

"Not everyone sees ribbons and thinks they're a suggestion," I quipped, though I had to admit it wasn't the most secure setup.

Nick gave me a reassuring pat on the shoulder. "It's fine for now. The police will handle it when they get here."

Still, a faint sense of unease lingered as Paula reappeared, her clipboard in hand and her demeanour resolutely composed. "I've spoken with the rest of the staff, and they're staying away from this side of the hall until further notice."

"Thanks, Paula," I said, though my mind was still racing with questions about Beatrice and the strange reactions we'd seen from Charles and Melinda.

"I know this isn't how you pictured today going," Paula continued, offering a sympathetic smile. "But since we've got some time before Wiggles arrives, how about I show you the rest of the hall? It might help take your mind off things."

I hesitated, glancing at Nick, who gave a small nod of encouragement. "That sounds like a good idea," I said finally. If nothing else, it would give me a chance to ask Paula about Beatrice—and her family—without seeming too obvious.

Paula led us through a set of grand double doors into what she called "The Sunroom," though the name felt a bit optimistic in the current winter gloom. Still, the room had a certain charm, with tall arched windows that overlooked the snow-covered gardens and warm, glowing lanterns that chased away the shadows.

"As you can see, the sunroom can be used for drinks receptions or smaller ceremonies," Paula explained. "It's a popular choice in the spring, but for winter weddings, it's more of a spill-over space."

"It's lovely," I said, my eyes lingering on a pair of antique armchairs near the window. "Paula, can I ask... what was Beatrice like? I mean, as a person?"

Paula's steps faltered slightly, and for a moment, I worried I'd overstepped. But she recovered quickly, her expression thoughtful. "Beatrice was... complicated. She was fiercely intelligent, always the sharpest person in the room. But she could also be guarded, especially after her mother passed."

"She inherited the hall from her mother, didn't she?" Nick asked.

Paula nodded. "Yes. Beatrice was the favourite—everyone knew it. Her mother doted on her. When she passed away, Beatrice took over the hall. She threw herself into it completely, almost as if she were trying to prove something."

"What about the rest of her family?" I asked casually, trying to sound more curious than investigative. "I met Charles and Melinda earlier, but I didn't get much of a sense of them."

Paula let out a soft sigh. "Melinda isn't family."

I gasped. "She's not?"

"That's Melinda North. She's Beatrice's executive assistant."

"She seemed so confident with Charles, not to mention she showed more emotion about Beatrice's death."

Paula rocked back on her feet, her discomfort palpable. "Charles is different, I'm aware of that. He always felt like he was living in Beatrice's shadow. He never cared for the family business—he's more interested in his own ventures. Melinda, on the other hand, has always been Beatrice's closest ally. She was practically the hall's co-manager."

"Why has nobody missed Beatrice?" I pressed gently.

"Yes, that's curious," Paula said, her brow furrowing

slightly. "Beatrice told us she'd be travelling for the holidays. She went somewhere, Bali I believe, somewhere fancy like that. She needed time to work through her grief."

"You don't seem too sure about that as an idea," Nick said with an encouraging smile.

"Oh, I'm very sure about it as an idea. In fact, as an idea, I think everyone should be able to take time to work through their grief."

"You wanted time off, too," I realised.

Paula jolted back and shook her head, her neat hair barely moving. "Absolutely not. I happily dedicate my life to the hall. It's just, well, Mrs Harper is deeply missed by the staff here. I'd like to see their grief recognised a little, that's all."

Nick and I exchanged a quick glance, though we didn't comment. Paula led us through another doorway into the dining hall, a grand space dominated by a long oak table and an ornate chandelier.

"This is where the wedding breakfast will take place," Paula said, her tone brightening. "We'll have the table set with gold runners, festive centrepieces, and, of course, your housekeeper will have input."

"Gilbert? He will?" I asked.

Paula raised her eyebrows. "Oh yes, Holly. He's been *very* clear that he must be consulted on every detail, no matter how tiny."

Nick let out a laugh. "That sounds like Gilbert. I hope he won't be too much trouble for you."

Her expression turned pensive. "Beatrice was something of a perfectionist too. She had a reputation for being demanding, but I think she just wanted everything to live up to her vision."

As Paula spoke, I couldn't shake the feeling that there

was more to Beatrice's story than she was letting on. The way she spoke about Beatrice and her family felt carefully curated, as though she were choosing her words with great care.

"Paula," I said slowly, "do you think Beatrice would have had any enemies? Anyone who might have wanted to harm her?"

Paula froze mid-step, her eyes darting towards mine. For a moment, she looked like she wanted to say something, but then her shoulders sagged slightly. "I don't know," she said finally. "Beatrice was complicated, like I said. She had high expectations and could be... blunt. That didn't always sit well with people. But harm her? I can't imagine it."

Her words lingered as we finished the tour, my thoughts spinning with the fragments of information she'd shared. Beatrice had been brilliant and driven, but also guarded and demanding. What secrets had she been keeping—and who might have wanted to silence her?

3

———

The dining hall of *The Olde Jolly Hall* was breathtaking, a space steeped in grandeur. The polished oak table stretched the length of the room, its surface gleaming under the light of an ornate chandelier that sparkled like icicles. The air smelled faintly of pine and cinnamon, though the festive warmth of the decorations felt at odds with the tension crackling in the air.

Charles Harper stood at the far end of the room, his hands stuffed into the pockets of his tailored trousers. His expression was unreadable, though his posture—rigid, almost confrontational—made it clear he wasn't happy to be there.

"It's not as though I came running, Paula," Charles said, his tone clipped. "I had important work to attend to. This entire... situation feels exaggerated. What was that woman even doing looking into our passageways?!"

Paula, standing near the doorway with her clipboard held protectively against her chest, shot him a withering glare. "With all due respect, Charles, your sister was found dead in your family's hall. I think that qualifies as serious."

Nick and I exchanged a quick glance. We were seated near the middle of the long table, trying to appear unobtrusive while still gathering as much information as we could. So far, it wasn't difficult; Charles wasn't exactly subtle about his feelings.

Melinda North stood near the windows, her arms crossed tightly over her chest. Her composed demeanour was cracked, her lips pressed into a thin line as her gaze flitted between Charles and Paula.

"It's almost as if you're happy," Melinda said, her voice barely above a whisper.

Charles gave out a bitter laugh. "Happy?! Happy? You've got no idea the headache this will be to sort out."

"She's dead, Charles, there is no sorting it out," Paula's voice was grim.

"*I* don't know how Beatrice ended up here," Charles said, exhaling sharply. "As far as *I'm* concerned, she was in Bali."

"That's the part I don't understand," I said, keeping my tone gentle. All eyes turned toward me, and I hesitated only briefly before continuing. "How could Beatrice have been emailing and updating you if she... if she's dead?"

Charles' green eyes narrowed slightly, though there was no real emotion behind them. "You don't strike me as a detective, Miss Wood."

"She's very good at asking questions," Nick said, his tone even as he leaned back in his chair. "You should try answering her."

"I beg your pardon?" Charles' voice sharpened, but Melinda stepped in before the conversation could escalate further.

"Let's all take a breath, shall we?" she said, her voice calm but edged with fatigue. "This isn't helping anything."

Charles met her gaze, smiled, and mouthed *thank you*. Interesting.

I studied Melinda closely, noting the faint tremor in her hand as she brushed a stray strand of hair from her face. Her polished exterior was intact, but barely. The cracks were showing.

"Melinda," I said softly, "you were close to Beatrice, weren't you?"

Her eyes flicked toward me, startled. "I—I suppose you could say that. We worked together every day and I had a great deal of respect for her. Beatrice was... driven."

"That's one word for it," Charles muttered, earning a sharp glare from Paula.

"She pushed people," Melinda continued, ignoring Charles. "Sometimes too hard. But she had a vision for this hall, and she never let anything—or anyone—stand in her way."

The weight of her words settled over the room like a thick fog. I could see Paula shift uncomfortably, her knuckles whitening as she clutched her clipboard. Charles looked distinctly bored, as though the discussion was beneath him.

"What about her family?" I asked, directing my question toward Charles this time. "Did you support her vision?"

"Support is a strong word," he replied, his tone dripping with sarcasm. "Beatrice didn't exactly invite collaboration. She was the queen bee, always in charge, always right."

"That must have been difficult for you," I said, keeping my voice neutral.

He shrugged. "It's easier to step aside than fight with someone like her. She had the inheritance, the hall, the power. The rest of us were just pieces on her chessboard."

I caught a flicker of something in Melinda's expression

—disapproval, maybe, or frustration—but it vanished as quickly as it appeared.

"And what about you, Melinda?" I pressed. "Did Beatrice's 'vision' ever clash with yours?"

Melinda hesitated, her eyes darting toward Paula as though seeking permission to speak. Paula gave her a small nod, and Melinda exhaled softly.

"Beatrice and I worked well together," she said finally. "But... she wasn't without her flaws. She could be... difficult."

"Difficult enough for someone to want to harm her?" Nick asked bluntly, his gaze fixed on Charles.

Charles scoffed, leaning casually against the wall. "Oh, please. Beatrice had enemies—I won't pretend otherwise. But most of them were professional. Competitors with their crazy low offers to scoop up this place. Contractors. That sort of thing. No one in the family would stoop to murder."

"Competitors?" I echoed, frowning. "Was she planning to sell the hall?"

"No," Melinda said quickly, her tone firm. "Beatrice would never sell. The hall was her life."

"More than her family was, apparently," Charles added, his voice laced with bitterness.

The tension in the room was almost palpable now, the unspoken accusations and old resentments swirling around us like a winter storm. Paula, sensing the conversation was spiralling, stepped forward.

"Enough," she said, her voice steady but firm. "This isn't solving anything. The police will be here soon, and I suggest we all cooperate fully when they arrive, but there's nothing to be gained by us fighting like a group of children."

Charles straightened, his expression unreadable. "Of course. Anything to clear up this mess quickly."

With that, he strode toward the doorway, pausing only briefly to glance over his shoulder. "You might want to focus on your wedding, Miss Wood. This murder business doesn't suit you."

The doors closed behind him with a soft thud, leaving a heavy silence in his wake.

Melinda sighed, rubbing her temples. "I'll... I'll check in with the staff," she muttered, excusing herself quickly.

Paula lingered, her clipboard held tightly against her chest. "I'm sorry about him," she said softly. "Charles has always been... complicated."

"Complicated is putting it mildly," Nick said, his jaw tight.

I nodded absently, my mind racing with everything we'd just heard. Beatrice's vision, her control, her enemies—there were so many threads to untangle. And Charles... his indifference felt almost too practiced.

As Paula left to attend to other matters, Nick turned to me. "What do you think?"

"I think Charles is hiding something," I said. "And Melinda's nervous about more than just the murder."

Nick nodded. "We'll figure it out. But be careful, Holly. These people... they've got more secrets than Christmas presents under the tree."

I managed a small smile at his attempt to lighten the mood, but the weight of the mystery loomed large in my mind. Beatrice's death wasn't just a tragic accident—it was the spark that could set the entire Harper family alight.

**

I found Gilbert in the kitchen, orchestrating what could only be described as a culinary battlefield. The normally serene space had been transformed into a bustling hub of activity, with staff dashing between counters laden with bowls, trays, and piping bags. Aromas of cinnamon, chocolate, and warm pastry mingled in the air, creating a tantalising symphony that almost made me forget that there was a body in a passageway not too far from us.

"Brush! Don't drizzle! Am I speaking another language?" Gilbert's voice cut through the clatter of pots and pans as he pointed a whisk like a baton at a nervous sous chef. "The cranberry glaze must be brushed—lightly, delicately, as if you're painting the ceiling of the Sistine Chapel. Do you want these police officers thinking they've stumbled into a roadside café?"

The sous chef muttered an apology and got back to work, her cheeks flushed. Two other staff members stood by, hastily preparing an array of tiny sandwiches and miniature mince pies under Gilbert's watchful eye.

"What's all this?" I asked, stepping into the room. "Surely the Hall doesn't have an event on today?"

Gilbert turned, his expression brightening slightly when he saw me. "Ah, Holly, thank goodness you're here! Someone with sense. These cooks clearly need supervision and leadership."

Before I could answer, Gilbert turned to face the harried team and called out, "Isn't that right?"

"Oui, chef!" The team answered in a perfect synchrony which I suspected Gilbert had made them practice until perfect.

I arched a brow. "Seriously, Gilbert, what is this? If there are guests coming, we'll have to cancel them. This place is a crime scene."

"You're not wrong. A kitchen this sloppy is a crime scene for sure, but I've sorted that, don't worry." Gilbert waved a hand at the spread. "This is a gesture of goodwill, my dear. A show of hospitality for the fine officers who will undoubtedly be interrogating us about the body you found in the passageway. If there's one thing I know, it's that a well-fed investigator is a less irritable investigator."

"Or a distracted one," I muttered, though I couldn't help smiling. "You think feeding them cranberry-glazed pastries will help them solve the case?"

"I think feeding them cranberry-glazed pastries will make them less likely to shout at me when I inevitably tell them what they're doing wrong," Gilbert replied, his tone dripping with mock innocence. "Now, do sit. I need your opinion on these."

Before I could protest, he grabbed a plate of dainty éclairs from the counter and placed them in front of me. Each one was a miniature work of art, with glossy chocolate ganache and a delicate dusting of powdered sugar.

"Go on," he urged. "Tell me they're perfect."

I picked one up, the cool ganache giving way to a rich, creamy filling as I took a bite. "They're perfect," I admitted, though I knew he didn't need my validation.

"Of course they are," he said, preening. "Now, tell me— what have you uncovered so far? Surely you've gotten more out of Charles and Melinda than the police will."

"Charles is evasive, Melinda is nervous, and Paula is exhausted," I said, ticking them off on my fingers. "But none of that explains why Beatrice was killed."

Gilbert nodded thoughtfully, leaning back against the counter. "The staff have their own theories, of course. Plenty of chatter about Beatrice's recent... let's say, eccentricities."

My ears perked up. "Eccentricities? Like what?"

"Well," he said, lowering his voice and glancing at the busy staff, "she'd been keeping odd hours, locking herself away in the study for days at a time. One of the housekeepers swears she overheard her on the phone, talking about 'exposing the truth.'"

"Exposing the truth?" I repeated, setting down the éclair. "Did they say anything else?"

Gilbert eyed the plate before me with a frown. "Are you not finishing that? What's wrong with it? I'll have you know that that chocolate was tempered to perfection, I didn't even blink while I was making it, and you take a bite and discard it? Why, I've got a good mind to hang up my..."

I grabbed the eclair and stuffed the rest of it into my mouth in one, making sure to make appreciative groans as I chewed.

Gilbert gave a one-sided smile and winked at me. "That's better. There's not much more to say, really. Only that Beatrice seemed increasingly agitated in the weeks before her disappearance—or death, as it were. The rest of it is conjecture, of course. Staff gossip is an art form, but it's rarely reliable."

"Still," I said, my mind racing, "if Beatrice was working on something significant, it could explain why someone wanted her silenced."

Gilbert nodded. "Exactly what I was thinking. Though, if you ask me, this is less about the hall and more about her family. Have you noticed how Charles and Melinda can barely tolerate being in the same room? Every time she's near, he ups and leaves."

I nodded as I leaned against the counter, my thoughts swirling. Beatrice's inheritance, her relationship with Charles and Melinda, and now this cryptic reference to exposing the truth—it was all starting to feel like pieces of a much larger puzzle.

"I need to speak to the staff directly," I said, my voice

firm. "If Beatrice was working on something, they might know more."

Gilbert nodded approvingly. "A wise decision. Just be prepared for a lot of 'I heard this from so-and-so.' People love a scandal."

I smiled faintly. "Noted. In the meantime, have you had chance to think of any wedding things? I'm guessing the cranberry glaze is something of a test run."

Gilbert sighed dramatically, gesturing to the chaos around him. "The menu will be flawless—naturally—but don't get me started on the floral arrangements. If that florist doesn't show up tomorrow with the peonies I specifically ordered, I might have to commit a murder of my own."

"Let's not add to the police workload," I said, laughing. "Anything else?"

"The seating arrangements are a disaster," he declared, throwing up his hands. "Paula had had an attempt, of course, bless her heart, but I tore the whole thing up and started over. Trying to balance magical guests with human ones is an impossible task. If Mrs Claus and Betty end up at the same table, we'll never get through the speeches."

"Betty? The reindeer?" I asked, stifling a laugh.

"Of course, Betty. Lovely as she is, she'll spend the entire evening critiquing everyone's perfume choices. She's something of a diva, that one."

"I trust you to make it work," I said, still laughing. "If anyone can pull this off, it's you."

"Flattery will get you everywhere, darling," Gilbert said, grinning. Then his expression turned more serious. "But let me worry about the wedding. You've got bigger things to focus on—like solving a murder before you walk down the aisle."

His words sent a chill through me, despite the warmth of the kitchen. "No pressure, right?"

"None at all," he said breezily, turning back to the counter. "Now, off you go. I have éclairs to perfect and detectives to impress."

I smiled, shaking my head as I left the kitchen. Gilbert's antics had done a decent job of lifting my spirits, but the weight of his revelation still pressed on me. Beatrice's death wasn't random. There was a reason she'd been killed, and I was determined to find out what it was—before her secrets jeopardised more than just my wedding day.

4

———

The main hall was alive with a flurry of activity. Staff bustled about, carrying garlands, candles, and boxes of glittering ornaments. The festive air smelled of pine and cinnamon, but the atmosphere was anything but calm. The soft murmur of Christmas hymns playing from a speaker in the corner was drowned out by the sharp, unmistakable voice of a certain elf.

"Stop! Step away from the wreath, Carol. Step. Away." Gilbert darted toward one of the staff, his hands fluttering like an overexcited conductor. "You've tied the bow too tightly. Do you want the poor thing to suffocate?"

The young woman stepped back, looking both confused and apologetic. "I thought tighter bows were better?"

"For what? Strangling cherubs?" Gilbert clutched his chest in mock agony. "No, no, no, darling. Bows should be airy, inviting, and festive. Here, watch and learn." With a dramatic flourish, he undid the bow and began retying it, each motion precise and delicate. "There we go. See? She's breathing again."

I bit back a smile as I watched him. Gilbert might have been exacting, but there was no denying his dedication. He was a man on a mission—a mission to make my wedding the most magical event of the century.

He stepped back to admire his handiwork, then caught sight of me standing by the door. His face lit up instantly. "Holly, thank goodness you're here. I've been carrying the weight of this entire operation on my back, and it's starting to give me posture issues."

"Gilbert," I said, walking toward him, "you know you don't have to do this all on your own. The staff are perfectly capable of decorating."

He gasped, clutching the bow he'd just tied as though I'd insulted his honour. "Capable? Holly, this isn't just decorating. This is art. This is ambiance. This is setting the stage for the most important day of your life! You deserve more than capable. You deserve perfection."

"I appreciate that," I said, smiling, "but I don't want the staff to stage a mutiny."

"They wouldn't dare," Gilbert replied with a wink. "They know I'm doing this out of love. Isn't that right, everyone?"

A chorus of murmured agreement rose from the staff, who were all valiantly trying to keep up with his high standards. I couldn't help but laugh.

Nick sauntered in from the side of the hall, his hands stuffed into his pockets. "Looks like you've got everything under control here, Gilbert."

"Under control?" Gilbert turned to him with an incredulous expression. "Nick, darling, control is for amateurs. This is a finely orchestrated symphony of glitter and greenery. If I weren't here, they'd have turned this place into a second-rate carol service backdrop."

Nick smirked. "And we can't have that."

"Exactly," Gilbert said, adjusting a centrepiece. "Now, Holly, you must approve these table settings. I've tested three variations, and I need you to tell me which one sings to your soul."

He led me to a nearby table, where three identical-looking place settings were laid out. I studied them carefully, though I couldn't for the life of me see any real difference. As far as I could tell, each one featured pristine white china plates edged with delicate gold filigree, each paired with polished silver cutlery and a crystal glass shimmering under the chandelier's light. A folded crimson napkin, tucked into a gold napkin ring shaped like a holly wreath, sat neatly atop each plate, accompanied by a single sprig of evergreen for a festive touch.

"Um... they're all lovely," I said diplomatically.

"Lovely?" Gilbert frowned. "Holly, please. This is your wedding. 'Lovely' is for baby showers and retirement parties. Which one makes your heart flutter?"

I squinted, then pointed at the middle setting. "That one, I guess?"

"Excellent choice!" Gilbert said, clapping his hands together. "I knew you had taste."

Paula appeared at my side, clipboard in hand and an amused smile on her face. "He's been like this all morning," she said under her breath. "I'm amazed no one's thrown a bauble at him yet."

"He means well," I said, watching as Gilbert began rearranging the napkins with the focus of a surgeon. "He just wants everything to be perfect."

"For you," Paula added with a knowing smile. "It's sweet, in a slightly terrifying way."

Across the hall, one of the staff struggled to hang a

garland above the fireplace, the heavy greenery slipping from her grasp. Gilbert swooped in like a festive superhero, catching the garland before it could fall.

"Careful, Susan! This isn't a tug-of-war match," he said, adjusting the garland with deft hands. "There. Now it's perfectly draped. Remember, darling, gravity is your friend, not your enemy."

"Thanks, boss," Susan said, looking both relieved and amused.

I walked over to him, folding my arms. "You know, Gilbert, you're making everyone nervous."

"Nervous? They're learning," he replied, stepping back to admire his work. "I'm an educator at heart, Holly. A mentor. A bringer of beauty."

"A bringer of stress, more like," I teased. "But I get it. You want this to be perfect."

"Of course I do," he said, his voice softening. "This is your wedding, Holly. The moment you and Nick start your forever. How could I settle for anything less?"

His sincerity caught me off guard, and for a moment, I felt a lump rise in my throat. "Thank you, Gilbert," I said quietly. "It means a lot."

He waved a hand dismissively, though his eyes were bright. "Don't get all mushy on me, darling. I'll start crying, and then the ribbons will end up crooked."

Nick walked over, slinging an arm around my shoulder. "He's got a point. Crooked ribbons would ruin the whole day."

"You're not helping," I said, nudging him playfully.

Gilbert straightened, clapping his hands together. "All right, enough chit-chat. Back to work, everyone! We've got candles to place and wreaths to fluff. No slacking!"

As the staff scurried back to their tasks, I couldn't help

but smile. Gilbert might have been a loveable, sassy diva, but his heart was as big as the Christmas tree standing in the corner. And while his high standards might have driven everyone a little mad, I knew he was only pushing so hard because he cared.

**

The main hall had settled into a quieter rhythm as the staff moved on to fine-tuning the decorations. Gilbert, mercifully preoccupied with inspecting the arrangement of fairy lights on the staircase, left Paula and me free to chat near the grand Christmas tree.

Paula adjusted the clipboard in her hands, her expression thoughtful as she watched the staff work. "I'll say this for Gilbert," she said, glancing at me with a faint smile. "He certainly has an eye for detail."

"An eye, a megaphone, and a flair for dramatics," I replied, chuckling. "But he has a good heart, hidden in there somewhere underneath all the perfectionism!"

Paula nodded, her gaze drifting to the fireplace where Susan was carefully re-fluffing the garland in line with Gilbert's earlier instructions. "Perfection is a high bar. Especially when there are... complications."

I tilted my head, sensing a weight in her tone. "Complications like the Harper family?"

Paula let out a soft sigh, her shoulders slumping slightly. "It's not easy, working with a family as... layered as the Harpers."

I gestured toward the seating area near the tree, and we both sat down on the plush red armchairs, the flickering light from the chandelier casting a soft glow over us. "I noticed some tension earlier," I said carefully. "Especially between Charles and Melinda. And Charles didn't seem particularly... affected by Beatrice's death."

Paula pursed her lips, her clipboard resting on her lap as she considered her words. "Charles has always been complicated. He and Beatrice were... let's just say they weren't close."

"Why not?" I asked, leaning forward slightly.

Paula hesitated, then sighed again. "Beatrice was their mother's favourite. Everyone knew it—Charles included. When their mother passed, it was no surprise that she left the hall to Beatrice. But it didn't sit well with Charles. He felt slighted, overshadowed."

I frowned. "Overshadowed? By Beatrice?"

Paula nodded. "Beatrice was... larger than life. She had this presence, this drive. She took the hall's legacy very seriously, and she was determined to make it something extraordinary. But Charles... he never wanted any of it. Not the hall, not the responsibility, not the expectations."

"So why would he feel slighted?" I asked, trying to piece it together.

Paula gave me a small, sad smile. "Because their mother's attention wasn't about what they wanted. It was about who she thought was worthy. Beatrice was 'the chosen one,' in their mother's eyes. And Charles... well, he always felt like the forgotten child."

"That must have been hard for him," I said softly.

"It was," Paula agreed. "But instead of finding his own path, he stayed here. He worked under Beatrice's shadow, resenting her but refusing to leave. It created this... bitterness between them. They didn't fight openly, but the tension was always there."

I glanced toward the far end of the hall, where Charles had disappeared earlier. "Do you think he hated her?"

Paula hesitated again, her brow furrowing. "I don't know if 'hate' is the right word. But I think he blamed her for a lot of things—things that weren't really her fault. And Beatrice... well, she didn't exactly go out of her way to make him feel included."

The pieces were beginning to fall into place. Charles' indifference to Beatrice's death, his clipped tone when discussing her, his bitterness about the inheritance—it all pointed to a strained relationship that went far deeper than sibling rivalry.

"Do you think Charles could have hurt her?" I asked quietly.

Paula's eyes widened slightly, and she looked down at her clipboard, fidgeting with the edge of the paper. "I don't want to believe that. But... I don't know. There's a lot of history there. A lot of unresolved resentment."

I nodded, my thoughts racing. Charles had a motive, that much was clear. But was resentment enough to drive him to murder? Or was there something more—something deeper—fuelling his actions?

As Paula shifted uncomfortably in her seat, Gilbert appeared behind us, holding a sprig of mistletoe like a sceptre. "Ladies, I hate to interrupt your little tête-à-tête, but there's a crisis unfolding by the dessert table. Someone had the audacity to suggest adding powdered sugar to the mince pies."

Paula and I exchanged a glance, then burst out laughing. Gilbert looked between us, bemused. "I fail to see what's so funny," he said, his voice rising a pitch. "This is a matter of culinary integrity!"

I stood, wiping a tear from the corner of my eye. "Let's go save the pies before Gilbert starts filing grievances."

As we walked toward the dessert table, the laughter faded, and Paula's words lingered in my mind. Charles' bitterness toward Beatrice was a powerful thread in this tangled web of secrets and lies. But whether it was the thread that would unravel the truth... that remained to be seen.

5

———

The kitchen was in chaos again. Not the productive, festive chaos of earlier, with garlands being hung and place settings debated. This was full-blown Gilbert-level chaos. Pots clanged, wooden spoons were flung aside in frustration, and the unmistakable sound of an exasperated huff punctuated the air.

"Cranberries!" Gilbert's voice bellowed, reverberating through the hall like an outraged town crier. "These are not cranberries. These are tiny, shrivelled impostors masquerading as cranberries."

I entered the kitchen cautiously, taking in the scene. A bag of the offending berries lay discarded on the counter, spilling their tart little bodies across the polished surface. Gilbert stood over them like a general surveying a battlefield, his hands planted firmly on his hips. His apron, pristine as always, was slightly askew—a sure sign that his patience had reached its limit.

"Gilbert," I began, stepping closer. "What's going on?"

"What's going on?" he repeated, his voice rising dramatically. "What's going on, Holly, is a travesty of epic proportions! These—these abominations—are meant to be served at *your* wedding. I'd rather resign on the spot than be associated with such mediocrity."

One of the kitchen staff, a young man with flour smudged across his apron, glanced at me helplessly. "We tried sourcing the organic cranberries Gilbert requested, but the supplier didn't have any left. We thought these would be fine—"

"Fine?" Gilbert cut in, his eyes wide with disbelief. "*Fine* is for corner cafés and packet stuffing. This is not just a wedding, it is *the* wedding of the century, and I will not allow substandard produce to tarnish my reputation—or Holly's memories!"

The poor staff member mumbled an apology and hurried off, leaving me to handle the culinary diva before me. I crossed my arms and gave Gilbert a pointed look. "Gilbert, you've got to calm down. They're just cranberries."

He gasped, clutching the edge of the counter for support as though I'd personally insulted his family. "Just cranberries? Holly, please. Do you think Monet said, 'It's just paint'? Or that Mozart shrugged off a poorly tuned piano? Cranberries are the foundation of the festive menu! They must be flawless!"

I sighed, glancing at the tray of half-finished canapés on the counter. "Gilbert, come on. You've faced bigger challenges than this. Remember last Christmas, when Mrs Claus accidentally set the pudding on fire, and you had to whip up a replacement in under ten minutes?"

"That was different," he huffed, straightening his apron. "That was a culinary miracle. This is sabotage."

Suppressing a smile, I walked over to the counter and grabbed a plate of freshly baked gingerbread. "Sit," I said, gesturing toward the small table in the corner. "Have some tea and a gingerbread man. You can't save the menu on an empty stomach."

"I'm not hungry," he protested, though his eyes betrayed him as they darted toward the plate.

"Gilbert," I said, fixing him with my best no-nonsense look, "sit."

He sighed dramatically but obeyed, sinking into a chair as though the weight of the world rested on his shoulders. I poured him a steaming cup of tea from the pot on the counter and placed it in front of him, along with the gingerbread. He picked up the biscuit with a mournful expression, as though it were a consolation prize for his dashed cranberry dreams.

"I just want everything to be perfect," he said softly, nibbling the edge of the gingerbread. "For you and Nick. You deserve that."

My annoyance melted away, replaced by a swell of affection. Beneath all his theatrics, Gilbert's heart was in the right place. He cared deeply, and his outrage over the cranberries wasn't just about his standards—it was about making my day as special as possible.

"I know you do," I said, sitting across from him. "And I appreciate it more than you know. But you don't have to carry all of this on your own. The staff are here to help, and so am I."

He took a sip of tea, his expression softening. "I suppose I might have been... a tad dramatic."

"A tad?" I teased, raising an eyebrow.

He chuckled, setting the cup down. "All right, maybe a touch more than a tad. But you have to admit, Holly—these cranberries are a crime against Christmas cuisine."

I laughed, reaching out to pat his hand. "We'll fix it. I'll call the supplier myself if I have to. But for now, let's work with what we've got. You can turn even the most ordinary ingredients into something extraordinary. You've done it before."

Gilbert sat up a little straighter, his ego clearly soothed by my confidence in him. "You're right. Of course, you're right. A true artist can rise above even the gravest of setbacks."

"Exactly," I said, smiling. "Now, are we good? You're not going to quit on me?"

He waved a hand dismissively. "Oh, don't be ridiculous. I couldn't possibly abandon you at a time like this. Besides, who else would ensure the table settings are aligned to within a millimetre?"

"Who indeed," I said, standing. "Come on. Let's tackle this menu together."

As Gilbert followed me back to the counter, his usual spark returning, I couldn't help but feel a sense of gratitude. Gilbert was working so hard to make my wedding as special as it could be, and yet my thoughts couldn't stay focused on the big day.

I had a murder to solve.

**

The kitchen was settling back into a steady rhythm after Gilbert's cranberry crisis, the staff moving with quiet efficiency as they prepped trays of canapés and festive desserts. Gilbert, his energy restored after tea and gingerbread, was now orchestrating the team like a maestro, though his tone had softened into something resembling encouragement rather than a battle cry.

"Lovely piping on those tarts, Angela," he said, pausing to inspect a tray of lemon meringues. "You're channeling your inner artist. Keep it up."

I smiled to myself, grateful that the storm had passed.

Gilbert's passion might be exhausting, but it was also infectious.

As I leaned against the counter, Paula entered, her clipboard as ever tucked under her arm. She caught my eye and gave a small nod. "Everything under control now?"

"For the moment," I replied, lowering my voice. "But let's not mention berries."

Paula chuckled and opened her clipboard. "Since we've got most of the menu finalised, let's review the flow of service for the reception dinner."

Gilbert immediately perked up, abandoning the lemon tarts in favour of the clipboard. "Ah, yes, the flow of service. Timing is everything, Paula. If those soufflés arrive a moment too soon, they'll deflate. And as for the chocolate fountains—"

"Fountains, plural?" Paula interrupted, raising a brow.

"Of course, plural," Gilbert said, looking scandalised. "You don't expect me to serve only milk chocolate, do you? White and dark are essential."

I exchanged an amused glance with Paula as she sighed and flipped a page on her clipboard. "We'll circle back to the fountains. For now, let's focus on the first course."

As Gilbert and Paula debated the nuances of soup garnishes, one of the younger staff members, a girl named Sara, hesitated nearby, clutching a stack of menus. She looked unsure of whether to interrupt, so I waved her over.

"Everything okay, Sara?" I asked gently.

"Yes, Mrs Wood. I mean, Miss Wood. I mean, Mrs Claus-to-be —I mean, Holly," she said, flushing. "I just thought you'd want to see the menu proofs before they go to print."

I took the stack from her, flipping through the beautifully designed pages. The menu was elegant, with each course written in swirling gold script. But as I scanned the dessert options, Sara spoke again, her voice hesitant.

"It's strange not seeing her name on there," she said softly.

I looked up, frowning. "Whose name?"

"Beatrice's," Sara said, shifting uncomfortably. "She always insisted her name be on everything—menus, invitations, you name it. She liked everyone to know she was in charge."

Gilbert glanced up from the clipboard, his sharp ears catching the tail end of the conversation. "In charge, indeed. She had quite the reputation for it, didn't she?"

Sara nodded. "She could be... intense. But she was excited about this year's gala. Said she had big plans."

My interest piqued. "Big plans? What kind of plans?"

Sara hesitated, glancing toward Paula for guidance. Paula gave her a small nod of encouragement. "Go on, Sara," Paula said. "You're not saying anything wrong."

"Well," Sara began, her voice lowering conspiratorially, "she mentioned something about making an announcement. She didn't tell us what it was, just that it would change everything."

"Change everything?" I repeated, leaning forward slightly. "Did she give any hints?"

Sara shook her head. "No, she was being really secretive about it. But it sounded important—like something she'd been working on for a long time."

Paula's brow furrowed as she crossed her arms. "That's odd. Beatrice was always open about her plans for the gala. She thrived on the attention. Why keep it a secret?"

"Maybe she wanted to surprise everyone," Sara offered, but then she began to cry. "Sorry, Ms Adams, forgive me. It's just, a few of us kitchen folk worried we were going to be let go."

"What made you think that?" I couldn't help but ask.

Sara glanced behind her anxiously. "Well, it's nothing really, and I'm not moaning, it's just, the wages have been a bit late. A bit short, too, sometimes."

Paula gasped. "Why didn't you tell me?"

Sara shook her head. "Gosh, no, we didn't want to be any bother. We thought it was just one of those things the first time, but then it was even later, and, well, last month it wasn't even half what it should have been."

"Sara, you sweet girl. You should have told me immediately. How many people have had this issue?"

"Well, I mean, everyone in here I think. But we're not moaning, Ms Adams, honest. We'd rather get half than nothing. If the hall's not doing well, we're happy to work for less. And whatever Beatrice had planned for the gala... well..."

"Like you said yourself Sara, she probably just wanted to surprise everyone," Paula said with a reassuring squeeze of Sara's shoulder.

"Or maybe she didn't want anyone to stop her," I said softly, more to myself than to anyone else.

The room grew quiet for a moment, the weight of my words settling over us like a snowfall. Whatever Beatrice's plans had been, they had clearly been significant. Significant enough to make her keep them hidden—and perhaps significant enough to get her killed.

"Sara," I said gently, "did Beatrice ever talk about what the announcement might be related to? The hall? The family?"

Sara shook her head again. "She didn't say. But she was stressed about it. More stressed than I've ever seen her."

I exchanged a glance with Paula, who looked equally puzzled. Gilbert, however, seemed unfazed as he returned to the tray of lemon tarts.

"Stress or no stress, it's no excuse for keeping secrets," he said lightly. "A good gala thrives on transparency—and a well-stocked canapé station, of course."

"Gilbert," I said, giving him a look.

"What?" he said innocently. "I'm just saying, secrets have a way of spoiling even the best-laid plans. And from what I hear, Beatrice had plenty of those."

I sighed, turning my attention back to Sara. "Thanks for telling me, Sara. If you think of anything else, let me know, okay?"

She nodded, her relief evident as she retreated back to the printing station. Paula lingered, her expression thoughtful. "What do you think this announcement could have been?"

"I don't know," I admitted. "But if it was big enough to stress her out, big enough to 'change everything,' it might be the key to understanding why she was killed."

Paula nodded slowly. "We should mention it to the police when they arrive."

"Agreed," I said. "But I'm not waiting for them to connect the dots. If Beatrice had plans for the gala, then there's a chance someone didn't want those plans to happen."

Gilbert, polishing off a gingerbread man, gave me a sly smile. "Darling, you've got that glint in your eye again. Please tell me you're not about to crawl back into any secret passageways."

"Not yet," I said, smiling faintly. "But if it helps solve this mystery before my wedding, I'll do whatever it takes."

6

———

The dining hall was quiet now, the hum of activity from earlier replaced by a tranquil stillness. I had hoped for a moment of peace to collect my thoughts, but as I moved toward the far end of the hall, a muffled voice caught my attention.

"I told you to leave it alone!" Charles' sharp tone cut through the silence, his words clipped with frustration.

I froze, stepping back into the shadows near a towering garland-draped column. The voice had come from a doorway leading to the study, its heavy oak door ajar just enough for me to hear.

"You can't keep burying your head in the sand, Charles," Melinda's voice replied, lower but no less tense. "This isn't going away."

"This is Beatrice's mess," Charles snapped. "She was always the one digging into things that didn't concern her. And look where it got her."

A shiver ran down my spine. I leaned slightly closer, careful not to make a sound. From my angle, I could just make out the edge of the room, the flickering glow of a fire casting long shadows across the walls.

"Don't you dare put this all on her," Melinda shot back, her tone biting. "She had every right to know the truth. We all did."

Charles let out a bitter laugh. "The truth? About what? That our family isn't as perfect as Mother liked to pretend? Newsflash, Melinda: no family is. Beatrice just liked having secrets to lord over us."

"This wasn't about control," Melinda hissed, her voice shaking slightly. "She wasn't trying to use it against you—she wanted to fix things."

"Fix things?" Charles repeated, his voice dripping with sarcasm. "How, exactly, do you 'fix' a centuries-old stain on the Harper name? You don't, Melinda. You let it die with the people who caused it."

There was a pause, the kind that stretched long and heavy with unspoken tension. I held my breath, straining to hear more.

"She wanted to tell everyone at the gala," Melinda said finally, her voice quieter now. "She thought it would... I don't know, clear the air. Make things better."

"Better?" Charles repeated, his voice thick with disbelief. "It would have destroyed everything, Melinda. The hall, our reputation—everything Mother worked for. Beatrice never thought about the consequences, only her self-righteous need to play saviour."

"That's not fair," Melinda said, her voice tight with barely contained emotion. "She was trying to protect us."

"Protect us?" Charles' voice rose again, the sharpness making me flinch. "From what? She was putting a target on her own back, and now look where we are. She's dead,

Melinda. She's dead because she couldn't leave well enough alone."

"And you blame me, don't you? You think I should have stopped her. For us."

"For us?"

"All of us!"

Charles let out a snicker. "I should find whoever killed her and buy them a drink. They managed to do what you couldn't. Shut her up!"

I peeked further around the column, catching a glimpse of Charles pacing by the hearth. His normally pristine suit was slightly rumpled, his tie loosened as though it had been tugged at during the argument. Melinda stood near the desk, one hand braced against the polished wood, her face pale in the firelight.

"Do you really believe that?" she asked softly, her voice almost a whisper. "That she deserved this?"

Charles stopped pacing, his back to her—and to me. For a moment, the silence was deafening. Then he spoke, his voice low and strained. "No. Of course not. But she should have known better."

"Known better than what?" Melinda pressed, stepping closer to him. "Than to challenge you? Than to stand up for what she believed in?"

"Than to stir up trouble!" Charles snapped, spinning around to face her. "Do you think Mother would have approved of any of this? Beatrice was obsessed with digging into the past, with airing dirty laundry that should have stayed buried. She had no right."

"She had every right," Melinda said fiercely. "This is her legacy as much as it's yours. And maybe she didn't want to spend her life guarding lies."

Charles' jaw tightened, his hands clenching into fists at his sides. "You're naïve if you think the truth would have set anyone free. It would have torn this family apart."

"It already has," Melinda shot back, her voice breaking slightly. "And now she's gone."

I pressed a hand to my chest, trying to steady my breathing. The pain in her voice was palpable, and for a moment, I almost felt like an intruder. But I couldn't look away, couldn't ignore the weight of their words.

"She wanted to make things better."

Charles let out a humourless laugh, running a hand through his hair. "Better? You think a public spectacle would have made things better? It would have ruined us."

Melinda stepped back, crossing her arms tightly over her chest. "You always cared more about appearances than anything else."

"And you always sided with her," Charles shot back. "No matter how reckless or foolish she was, you were always right there, feeding her delusions."

"I believed in her," Melinda said simply. "And I still do."

Their footsteps moved toward the doorway, and I quickly ducked back behind the garlanded column, my heart pounding in my chest. As they exited the study, their faces were tight with tension. Charles strode ahead, his jaw set, while Melinda lingered, her expression conflicted.

As they disappeared down the hallway, I emerged from my hiding spot, my mind racing. What had Beatrice discovered about their family's history? And why had it caused so much turmoil?

I glanced toward the study, the door still slightly ajar. My instincts urged me to follow the trail they had left behind. If Beatrice's discoveries were significant enough to spark this kind of argument—and potentially put her life in danger—then I needed to find out exactly what she had uncovered.

That would have to wait, though, because the peace was disturbed at that moment by a ring of the doorbell.

**

The melodic chime of the doorbell echoed through the hall, slicing through the stillness left behind by Charles and Melinda's heated argument. I froze mid-step. Who could it be? The police hadn't yet arrived, and I could only assume that Wiggles was still bogged down in his candy cane catastrophe.

Before I could make my way to the door, Paula appeared from the side corridor, clipboard clutched tightly against her chest. Her sharp heels clicked against the polished floor as she strode to the entrance, her expression shifting from puzzled to professional in an instant. I trailed behind her, curiosity pulling me along.

Paula tugged open the heavy oak door, letting in a gust of icy air that made the garlands on the walls flutter. A figure stepped inside, bundled in a long, tailored coat. Snowflakes clung to her dark hair, which framed a face that was strikingly beautiful and unmistakably young. Her cheeks were flushed from the cold, and her eyes, bright and curious, scanned the hall before landing on Paula.

"Evelyn!" Paula exclaimed, her surprise evident as she stepped back to allow the young woman inside. "We weren't expecting you."

Evelyn offered a sheepish smile as she unwound her scarf, revealing a sleek cashmere sweater beneath her coat. "I thought I'd surprise everyone. It's been too long since I've been here, and I assumed I'd have an invitation to the New Year Ball even though I failed to RSVP."

She slipped off her gloves and rubbed her hands

together for warmth, her gaze flitting around the hall. Her lips parted slightly as her eyes settled on the towering Christmas tree, her breath hitching for just a moment. When she noticed me, she gave a little wave.

I stepped forward, the urge to introduce myself overcoming my reluctance to intrude. "Hi, I'm Holly Wood," I said, offering my hand. "My fiancé, Nick, and I are getting married here in a few days."

Evelyn turned her attention to me, her smile widening as she took my hand in a firm, confident grip. "Holly, it's lovely to meet you. Congratulations! What a magical place for a wedding."

"Thank you," I said, studying her closely. There was an ease to her manner, but something beneath her cheerful exterior felt guarded.

Evelyn turned back to Paula, her tone becoming more casual. "Is Beatrice around? I wanted to catch up with her before things get too hectic."

Paula hesitated, her smile faltering for a fraction of a second before she regained her composure. "Beatrice isn't... available at the moment."

Evelyn tilted her head, her brow furrowing slightly. "Not available? Not even for her favourite baby sister?"

Ah. So Evelyn was a Harper sibling. The youngest.

"Not right now," Paula replied, her tone tight but polite. She looked at me in a panic, clearly unsure whether she should break the news or not.

As Paula spoke, Evelyn unbuttoned her coat, revealing perfectly tailored trousers and ankle boots that clicked softly against the polished floor as she moved toward the Christmas tree. She reached out, running her fingers lightly over one of the glittering ornaments, her expression wistful.

"There really is no place like this at Christmas time,"

Evelyn murmured quietly before returning her attention to Paula. "You don't think Charlie and Bea will mind terribly that I've just shown up like this? I promise not to cause any trouble."

Paula gave a weak smile. "You're always welcome here, you know that."

"Evelyn," I said. My voice was louder than I intended and I cringed at the way Evelyn jumped at my tone. "I'm afraid I need to tell you something. It's about Beatrice."

"She hasn't been herself lately," Evelyn said, her voice softening. "I noticed it the last time we spoke. Stressed, distracted. Has she seemed that way to you, too, Paula?"

Paula's grip on her clipboard tightened.

"There's no easy way to say this, but Beatrice is dead. I found her myself, just today. The police are on their way over here now."

Evelyn let out a small laugh, her fingers still toying with the ornament. "That's impossible."

"I know. It must feel that way. I'm so sorry."

"No, I won't believe it. Who even is this woman, Paula?"

Paula gave me an apologetic glance. "She's about to become Mrs Claus. Better watch your tone, love."

"No, no," I objected. I certainly didn't expect any preferential treatment from a grieving woman.

"We can't just let any random woman walk in here and tell us Beatrice is dead, Paula! What were you thinking? Where's Charlie? He won't put up with this rubbish!"

"Evelyn, I understand that this is a tremendous shock. I found your sister in a passageway in the Hall. It seemed like she'd been there for some time, I'm afraid."

She stepped back from the tree, turning to face us. Her smile returned, but it didn't quite reach her eyes. "Maybe you are telling the truth. This place doesn't feel the same without her energy."

I studied Evelyn carefully, my instincts prickling. Something about her words didn't sit right. "How often do you come to the hall?" I asked, trying to keep my tone light as I changed the subject from her sister's death.

"Not as often as I'd like," she admitted, crossing her arms. "I'm a student, you see. I used to come home every time I needed my laundry doing, but after Mummy died... well, it just wasn't the same."

Paula interjected quickly. "Why don't I take your coat, eh? You go on through to the sitting room. You must be frozen after your journey."

Evelyn hesitated for a moment, her gaze flicking toward the grand staircase before she handed Paula her coat. "Thanks, Paula. And don't worry, I won't get in the way. I thought it might be nice to spend a little extra time with the family this year. I didn't realise there'd be even fewer of us."

Her words hung in the air, and I felt the weight of what she didn't say. Before Paula could guide her away, Evelyn turned back to me. "Holly, what made you choose The Olde Jolly Hall for your wedding?"

"It felt magical," I said honestly, though my voice wavered slightly under her steady gaze. "Nick and I wanted something special, and this place seemed perfect."

She nodded thoughtfully. "It does have a certain charm, doesn't it? Beatrice worked so hard to keep it that way. She was always so determined."

The admiration in her tone was evident, but there was something else, too—something darker. I couldn't put my finger on it, but it was enough to make me uneasy.

Paula reappeared with a tray of tea and biscuits, expertly

balancing it as she set it down on a side table near the fire. "Here we are," she said brightly. "This should warm you right up."

Evelyn settled into one of the armchairs, tucking her legs beneath her as she reached for the tea. "Thank you," she said, her smile softening. "You always know how to make people feel at home, Paula."

"It's my job," Paula replied, though her eyes darted toward me for a brief moment, as if seeking reassurance.

I perched on the arm of the sofa, my thoughts still tangled in the undercurrents of Evelyn's arrival. "Do you always come home over Christmas?" I asked, hoping to keep the conversation going.

"I'd never been away over Christmas until this year," Evelyn admitted, blowing on her tea. "Gosh, now I wish I'd come sooner."

"You wouldn't have seen Beatrice if you had," Paula said quietly, arranging the biscuits on the tray. "We all thought she was in Bali."

Evelyn's gaze lingered on the fire, her fingers tightening around the teacup. "Oh, yes! How silly of me. I'd forgotten about her holiday."

Her words hung in the air like frost on a windowpane, delicate but unyielding. I felt a shiver creep up my spine as I watched her, the weight of her emotions simmering just beneath the surface.

"She never went, apparently," Paula said, her tone murky with confusion. "Or she went and came back. I don't know what to think, to tell you the truth."

"We will get to the bottom of it," I said.

"We?" Evelyn raised a perfectly sculpted eyebrow. Students sure looked a lot more glamorous nowadays than I ever had.

"The police, I mean."

"Hold on. If Bea really is dead, don't we need an ambulance? Or a coroner? Why are the police coming?"

"Well, it is a bit suspicious, Evelyn. You've got to admit that. We all think Beatrice is away in Bali, we're still getting our orders from her by emails, and it turns out she's been lying in some dusty passageway for who knows how long? It's not right!"

Evelyn frowned. "When you put it like that, it does sound odd. I didn't realise you were still hearing from her."

"Every day like clockwork," Paula explained. "Daily jobs, new bookings, changes to the website. She never could switch off, that one. She worked so hard."

"Maybe too hard," Evelyn replied, her smile returning, though it was faint. "I just hope it was worth it."

Before I could ask what she meant, a soft chime echoed through the hall—the clock on the mantel striking the hour. Evelyn glanced up, her expression brightening as though a switch had been flipped.

"Well," she said, setting her cup down and rising from the chair, "I should let you all get back to your preparations. I didn't mean to interrupt."

"You're not interrupting," Paula assured her, though her voice wavered slightly. "Make yourself comfortable. This is your home, too."

Evelyn's smile widened, but her eyes remained unreadable. "Thank you, Paula. And Holly—good luck with the wedding. I'm sure it'll be unforgettable."

Her words sent a ripple of unease through me, but I managed a polite smile. "Thanks. I hope you enjoy your time here."

As Evelyn left the room, her footsteps light and deliberate, I exchanged a glance with Paula. The older woman's face was drawn, her usual composure shaken.

"She's always been the quiet one," Paula said softly, almost to herself. "But quiet doesn't mean simple."

No, it didn't. And I was starting to suspect that Evelyn Harper's quiet demeanour concealed far more than she let on.

7

———

The study was quiet except for the faint crackle of the fire in the hearth. Shadows danced across the walls, playing over the heavy shelves crammed with leather-bound books and framed photographs. The air was thick with the scent of aged paper and polished wood, tinged with a faint trace of pine from the garland strung above the mantel. I paused at the door, hesitating before stepping inside.

The desk loomed in the centre of the room, a statement piece of furniture that seemed to hold an unspoken promise of secrets within its carved wooden frame. It was intimidating and alluring in equal measure. I swallowed hard and approached, the soft click of my boots on the hardwood floor barely audible over the steady rhythm of my breathing.

I pulled open the first drawer carefully, half expecting an alarm to sound or the ghost of Beatrice to appear, chastising me for intruding. Inside was a perfectly organised array of stationery, the kind that was too beautiful to use. Cream envelopes embossed with the Harper family crest, an ivory-handled letter opener, and a fountain pen that gleamed under the flickering firelight. Not a hair out of place, much like the Beatrice everyone described—precise, exacting, and entirely in control.

The second drawer held neatly filed papers, each folder labeled in her tidy script: *Accounts, Events, Staff Schedules.* It was all so... normal. Disappointingly normal. I bit my lip and moved to the third drawer, bracing myself for another round of hyper-organisation.

Instead, I found chaos.

The drawer was crammed with loose papers, crumpled receipts, and a stack of old invitations tied together with twine. It felt like an intrusion, rifling through the personal belongings of someone who could no longer defend their privacy. But if there was any hope of finding answers about her death, surely it lay in the mess Beatrice had hidden.

As I shifted through the contents, something fluttered out and landed at my feet. Bending to pick it up, I realised it was a photograph, creased and slightly faded with age. I straightened and turned it over, holding it close to the light.

The image was striking despite its wear. Beatrice stood in the foreground, her golden curls catching the sunlight, her confident smile as vivid as if she were standing before me now. Beside her stood a man I didn't recognise, his arm draped casually over her shoulder. His expression was harder to read—a mixture of warmth and caution, as though the moment had been stolen from him rather than offered freely.

I flipped the photograph over, and my breath caught. Scrawled across the back in sharp, dark ink were the words: *"The truth will set us free."* Below it, a date: *July 15th—just two weeks after her mother's death.*

I stared at the inscription, the weight of those words pressing down on me like the oppressive silence of the room. The truth. What truth? And why had it been so important to Beatrice? My mind raced with possibilities, each one more unsettling than the last.

Before I could delve deeper into the photograph's implications, my phone buzzed in my pocket, startling me. I fumbled to pull it out, my hands trembling slightly as Mrs Claus' name flashed across the screen. Her timing was impeccable.

"Hi, Mrs Claus," I answered, doing my best to keep my voice steady.

"Holly! How's my favourite bride-to-be? Is it all going well there, dear?" Her cheerful tone was like a warm embrace, a welcome reprieve from the shadows creeping around me.

I let out a soft laugh, though it felt hollow. "Surviving, I think."

"Surviving? Oh, no, no, no! You're supposed to be thriving! Now, tell me, have you finally picked a song for your first dance? Or are you still waffling between romantic ballads and something ridiculous from your university days?"

I chuckled despite myself, the memory of Nick's suggestion—*Jingle Bell Rock*—flashing in my mind. "Still waffling," I admitted. "But there's been a lot going on."

"Wedding planning can be a lot, dear," she said, her tone shifting to one of concern. "Are you all right? Is Nick taking good care of you?"

I glanced at the photograph in my hand, the cryptic words staring up at me like a challenge. "It's been... complicated. Beatrice Harper, the owner of the Hall, she's—well, she's dead. And I found her body. It's turned into a bit of a mystery."

The line went quiet for a moment, and I could picture

Mrs Claus frowning in concern on the other end. "Oh, Holly, that's terrible. Are you okay?"

"I'm fine," I said quickly, though the knot in my stomach suggested otherwise. "Nick's been amazing, as always. But I can't seem to stop thinking about it. There's something about her death—it doesn't add up."

"Well," Mrs Claus said thoughtfully, "if anyone can untangle a mystery, it's you. But don't let it consume you, Holly. Remember, you've got a wedding to plan. Don't let this derail everything."

"I won't," I promised, though the photograph in my hand begged to differ. "Actually, maybe you can help me think through something."

"Of course, dear. What's on your mind?"

I described the photograph, the man beside Beatrice, and the cryptic inscription. As I spoke, I found myself pacing the study, my free hand brushing over the smooth surface of the desk, trailing along the spines of books. Mrs Claus listened intently, her occasional murmurs of encouragement keeping me steady.

"That's certainly intriguing," she said when I finished. "It sounds like Beatrice was grappling with something big— something she felt compelled to share. And that man... he could be the key to understanding what was going on."

"That's what I was thinking," I said, pausing to glance at the desk again. "But where do I even start? There's no name, no clue about who he might be."

"Start with what you have," she advised. "The photo- graph, the date, the inscription—it's a trail, Holly. Follow it, and you'll find more pieces to the puzzle."

Her words filled me with a renewed sense of determina- tion. "You're right. Thanks, Mrs Claus. I'll let you know if I find anything."

"Good. And Holly?"

"Yes?"

"Don't forget to take a moment to breathe. And maybe think about that first dance song—you're running out of time!"

I laughed softly. "I'll try."

"As for me, I'm cooking up a storm while Gilbert isn't here to tell me off for messing up his kitchen!"

After hanging up, I turned back to the photograph, the firelight catching the edges of the creases. Mrs Claus was right—this was a trail, a breadcrumb left behind by Beatrice. The truth she had clung to so fiercely wasn't going to reveal itself, but if I followed her clues, maybe I could uncover it.

The question was whether I'd like what I found.

**

The front door burst open with a flurry of snow and a gust of icy wind, sending the warmth of the hall swirling upward toward the vaulted ceiling adorned with twinkling fairy lights. Wiggles stumbled in, his uniform askew and his cheeks flushed a rosy red that matched his bulbous nose. He wrestled with the stubborn door, finally managing to shut out the winter storm brewing outside.

"By the jingling bells of Saint Nicholas!" Wiggles exclaimed, stomping the snow from his boots onto the woven holly-patterned rug. "I've never seen such a candy cane catastrophe in all my years!"

I looked up from the plush armchair by the crackling fireplace, where I'd been sipping hot cocoa topped with a mountain of whipped cream and a dusting of cinnamon. Gilbert had insisted I sit and rest for a few moments with his signature drink.

"Wiggles, what's happened?" I asked, setting my mug

down on the side table adorned with a delicate lace doily and a sprig of mistletoe.

He hurried over, his eyes wide behind his wire-rimmed glasses, which were fogged from the sudden temperature change. "It's the elves at the North Pole distribution centre! A shipment of candy canes destined for the children's hospital got rerouted to the wrong continent! Can you imagine? Hundreds of candy canes meant to bring joy now sitting in a warehouse in Australia!"

Nick, who had been tending to the fire, turned with a sympathetic smile. "That's awful, Wiggles. But I'm sure they'll sort it out. There's no problem that Mitzy can't solve."

Wiggles huffed, pulling off his knit cap to reveal a mop of unruly silver hair. "I had to pull every string, call in every favour, and practically hitch a ride with a reindeer to get things back on track! But enough about that—I'm here now."

"Just in time, too," Gilbert chimed in as he breezed into the room, carrying a silver tray laden with freshly baked gingerbread cookies shaped like snowflakes and stars. The scent of molasses and spices filled the air, mingling with the pine from the garlands draped over the mantel.

"Ah, Gilbert, your timing is impeccable," Wiggles said, his eyes lighting up at the sight of the treats. "Don't mind if I do!" He reached for a cookie, then paused, noticing the tension in the room. "Am I interrupting something?"

I exchanged a glance with Nick, then held up the photograph I'd been clutching. "Actually, Wiggles, we could use your insight."

He settled into the overstuffed armchair opposite me, nibbling on the gingerbread. "Well, I'm all ears. What's on your mind, Holly?"

I handed him the photo. "I found this in Beatrice's desk.

It's her with an unidentified man, and there's an inscription on the back that says, 'The truth will set us free.' The date is shortly after her mother's death."

Wiggles adjusted his glasses, studying the image. "Hmm, intriguing. And you think this is connected to her... untimely demise?"

I nodded. Wiggles had directed a few junior officers to secure the entrance to the passageway where Beatrice laid. They would guard the area until the forensic pathologist arrived to examine the body. I shuddered at the thought of her, a recently vibrant and healthy young woman, transformed to being just a lifeless body.

Gilbert perched on the arm of the sofa beside me, his apron immaculate despite his endless baking. "I heard some things in the serving quarters about the old Mrs Harper's... extracurricular activities," he said with a clumsy attempt at a saucy wink.

"Gilbert!" I chided gently, though I wasn't sure whether I was more offended by his gossip or his weird facial expression. I also couldn't help but smile at his dramatics.

"Don't shoot the messenger, Holly!" he protested, tossing a peppermint candy into his mouth. "Rumour has it that Mr. Harper was away on 'business' for quite some time, and Mrs Harper found comfort elsewhere."

Wiggles leaned back, his gaze thoughtful. "Family secrets can be the heaviest burdens," he mused. "If Beatrice was uncovering something that someone wanted to keep hidden..."

"The man in the photo doesn't look exactly happy," Nick added, his arm resting protectively around my shoulders.

"Exactly," I agreed. "Whoever he is, Beatrice seems to have taken him by surprise. Or, well, it's like she's somehow making him do something he doesn't want to."

Wiggles nodded slowly, tapping a finger against the armrest. "You've met all of the Harper siblings? Let's just show them the photograph and see who the man is."

I nodded. "Evelyn was evasive and Charles is downright odd. I can't imagine that they'll tell us, even if they know who he is."

Gilbert snapped his fingers. "I could ask the servants."

Wiggles narrowed his eyes a little. "You do that, Gilbert, but be subtle. We'll see what they say, and then ask the Harpers."

Gilbert stood to attention and gave a mock salute as he took the photograph and held it as if it were the Crown Jewels. "I, sir, am nothing if not subtle."

With that, he turned and strode across the room towards the kitchen.

A log shifted in the fireplace, sending a shower of sparks up the chimney. The room fell silent for a moment, the weight of our suspicions settling over us like the snow blanketing the grounds outside.

"I hate to think ill of anyone," Wiggles began softly, "but if someone believed Beatrice was about to expose a secret that would shatter their world..."

"They might have felt desperate enough to stop her," I finished, the words heavy on my tongue.

"A family like this has so much to protect," Nick murmured. "The family history, the wealth. This isn't like your regular family fallout. The stakes must have felt very high."

"High enough to kill for," I said with a shudder.

Nick turned to me, his eyes filled with concern. "Are you sure you want to pursue this, Holly? We have the wedding in a few days..."

I placed a hand on his cheek, feeling the familiar roughness of his stubble. "I can't get married here knowing there's a dark cloud hanging over this place, and we'll never find another venue at such short notice. Beatrice deserves the truth to come out. And besides," I added with a small grin, "you didn't fall in love with me for my ability to sit on the sidelines."

He chuckled, pressing a kiss to my forehead. "No, I certainly didn't."

Wiggles cleared his throat, a twinkle in his eye. "Well then, it seems we have a mystery to solve. And if there's one thing I've learned, it's that nothing brings people together like a good old-fashioned sleuthing session."

Just then, the grandfather clock in the corner chimed, the deep notes resonating through the room. Outside, the snow continued to fall, blanketing the world in a pristine layer of white.

"Looks like we're in for a long night," I said, standing up and stretching. "Let's start by seeing if we can find out more about this man in the photo."

"Perhaps the attic holds some clues," Wiggles suggested. "Old family records, forgotten trunks..."

"Or the secret passages," Nick added with a mischievous grin. "You seem to have a knack for finding those."

I laughed, feeling a surge of excitement. "Then it's settled. We'll divide and conquer."

As we began to formulate our plan, Gilbert returned with steaming mugs of cider, the fragrant aroma filling the room. "To courage and camaraderie!" he declared, handing us each a mug.

We raised our mugs, the clink of them creating a harmonious note against the backdrop of the crackling fire and distant carollers whose voices carried on the wind.

"To uncovering the truth," I echoed.

And as we sipped the warm, spiced cider, I couldn't shake the feeling that we were on the cusp of unwrapping secrets that had been buried for far too long.

**

The kitchen was a symphony of controlled chaos, filled with the clatter of pots and the hiss of steam escaping from kettles. Aromas of cinnamon and nutmeg mingled with the savoury scent of roasting meat, creating a heady mix that wrapped itself around me as soon as I stepped in. Staff darted between stations, their movements quick and practiced as they worked to assemble the culinary delights for both the wedding menu and the upcoming holiday events.

Gilbert stood in the centre of it all, an island of theatrical energy amidst the bustle. He was orchestrating the scene with all the flair of a conductor leading an orchestra, pointing out errors with a dramatic flair that somehow felt endearing rather than overbearing.

"No, no, no!" he bellowed, waving a wooden spoon like a baton. "The rosemary sprigs are not to be *haphazardly tossed* on the roast! They must be *delicately placed*, as if you're adorning the crown of a queen!"

A young chef paused mid-sprinkle, looking as though he'd been caught committing a crime. Gilbert marched over, adjusted the sprigs himself with the precision of a jeweller, and then stepped back to admire his work.

"Better," he declared. "Though still not perfect. But I suppose perfection takes time, and I am but one man."

The staff exchanged weary but amused glances, clearly already accustomed to Gilbert's unique blend of exacting standards and over-the-top charm. One woman was rolling out dough for mince pies, her flour-dusted hands moving with quick efficiency. Another was carefully arranging tiny candied fruits onto a towering croquembouche, her tongue poking out slightly in concentration.

The air hummed with energy, the warmth of the ovens mingling with the occasional crisp burst of cold air as someone opened the door to retrieve a delivery. Somewhere in the background, a faint melody of Christmas carols played from a speaker, the cheerful jingles contrasting with the intensity of the work being done.

I approached Gilbert as he inspected a tray of canapés, his brow furrowed in concentration. "Gilbert, do you have a moment?"

"For you, my dear, always," he replied, though his eyes remained fixed on the canapés. "But make it quick—these are on the verge of perfection, and I mustn't let them linger too long in mediocrity."

I smiled as he handed me the photograph of Beatrice and the mystery man with as much stealth as any trained spy. "I've managed to ask a few trusted members of staff."

"And?"

Gilbert inclined his head to the left and back, then repeated the movement a few times. As a way of gesturing to indicate someone, it was about as far from subtle as he could be, but my gaze followed involuntarily. There was a wizened old elf in the corner of the kitchen, inspecting a huge bowl of cherries one by one. He had a single tooth which protruded from his lower lip over his top lip, and the bushiest eyebrows I had ever seen.

"Don't make it obvious you're looking!" Gilbert scolded me and I reluctantly dragged my gaze away from the old elf.

"Sorry. Who is that?"

"That's Horatio. He's the longest serving elf."

"Wow. The Olde Jolly Hall's longest serving elf! We should invite him to Claus Cottage for a celebratory lunch,"

I said, surprising myself with another little moment of thinking like a Claus.

But Gilbert simply rolled his eyes. "Longest serving elf in Candy Cane Hollow, not just at the hall. And don't invite him anywhere. He's not had a day off since 1952."

I laughed, but Gilbert simply eye-balled me. "You're being serious?"

Gilbert nodded. "He's from a different time. And he's got a good gig here. You see how he's sitting down on the job? A lot of places wouldn't allow that."

"He must know everything!" I exclaimed. A long-term member of household would be privy to all kinds of things!

"Oh, he does. But he's an old timer. Loyal to the family until death."

I winced at his choice of words. "Until whose death? His or his employer's?"

"His, of course. That was a silly question. Loyalty isn't something you owe a person only during their lifetime. Goodness, Holly, what did they teach you in school? Anyway. His loyalty was to his employer, the old Mrs Harper. He gets even a sniff of you trying to make her look bad and he'll close up quicker than a soft shell crab."

"So, what did he say?"

Gilbert burst into a hoot of laughter until tears streamed from his eyes. "Oh, no! No, you didn't! Holly, he won't tell me a single thing!"

I felt the disappointment in my stomach. "But... you said he knows everything."

"And he responds to power. Which I, as a lowly junior house elf when compared to his vast experience, have none. You, however..."

"You think he'll talk to me?"

"Almost certainly not. But it's worth a try."

I took a deep breath and squared my shoulders. Horatio didn't look particularly intimidating, but Gilbert's warning had me on edge. If he was as loyal as Gilbert claimed, there was a good chance I'd get nothing from him. Still, it was worth trying. I grabbed two mugs of steaming cider from the counter, their spicy aroma mingling with the heady scent of roasting chestnuts, and headed toward Horatio's corner.

He didn't look up as I approached, his gnarled fingers plucking cherries from the bowl with meticulous care. Each one received a thorough inspection before being placed in a neat row on the counter. Despite his age, his movements were steady, almost mechanical, and his brow furrowed in concentration beneath those formidable eyebrows.

"Horatio," I began, my voice light and cheerful, "I thought you might like a little something to warm you up."

He glanced at the mug I offered but didn't reach for it. "What's wrong with warming up by working?" His voice was deep and gravelly, carrying the weight of decades of experience.

"Well," I said, placing the mug carefully beside him, "sometimes it's nice to take a moment. Especially when you've been working as hard as you have."

He finally looked up, his sharp blue eyes peering out from beneath those bushy brows. "I don't take kindly to flattery, Miss."

I held up my hands in mock surrender. "Noted. But the cider's good, I promise."

He regarded the mug for a moment, then picked it up and took a cautious sip. His expression didn't change, but I caught the slightest nod of approval as he set it back down. Encouraged, I leaned against the counter, trying to appear casual.

"I hear you've been with the Harpers a long time," I said. "You must have seen everything."

"Seen a lot," he agreed, his tone neutral. "But seeing ain't the same as talking about it."

"Of course not," I said quickly. "I wouldn't ask you to share anything that wasn't appropriate. But I was hoping you might help me with something." I pulled the photograph from my pocket and placed it on the counter between us.

He glanced at it, his brows drawing together slightly. "What's this?"

"A photo I found in Beatrice's desk," I explained. "I don't recognise the man, but I thought maybe you might."

He picked up the photograph with surprising delicacy, holding it close to his face. For a moment, I thought I saw a flicker of recognition in his eyes, but he quickly masked it. "I'm afraid I can't help you."

"Are you sure?" I pressed gently. "The inscription on the back mentions the truth setting us free. It seems like something that was important to Beatrice."

Horatio set the photograph down, his expression unreadable. "Beatrice was always one for grand ideas. Liked to dig into things best left alone."

"Like what?" I asked, my voice soft. "Family history?"

He didn't answer right away, his gaze fixed on the cherries in front of him. When he finally spoke, his tone was measured, almost cautious. "Families like the Harpers have roots that run deep. Sometimes those roots tangle with things that should stay buried."

His words sent a shiver down my spine, though the room was warm. "Did Beatrice think something needed to be uncovered?"

Horatio's eyes flicked to mine, sharp and assessing. "You ask a lot of questions for someone who ain't family."

I hesitated, feeling the weight of his scrutiny. "Beatrice's death wasn't an accident," I said finally. "If there's something in her past—or the family's past—that could explain what happened, don't you think it's worth bringing to light?"

Horatio's jaw tightened, his hand curling slightly around the handle of his mug. For a moment, I thought he might send me away, but then he sighed deeply and leaned back in his chair.

"There was talk," he said slowly, his voice low. "Years ago, when the old Mr. Harper was away on business. Mrs Harper had a visitor—a man who came and went without much fuss. Didn't stay long, but long enough for people to notice."

My pulse quickened. "Do you know who he was?"

Horatio shook his head. "Didn't concern me. But some said he was an old friend. Others thought there was more to it."

"And Beatrice knew about him?"

Horatio's gaze turned distant, his fingers tapping absently against the mug. "If she did, she didn't say much. But she was always poking around, asking questions. Too many questions."

I leaned closer, lowering my voice. "Do you think this man could be the one in the photograph?"

Horatio didn't answer right away, his expression guarded. Finally, he pushed the photograph back toward me. "I don't know, and that's the truth. But if Beatrice was digging into old secrets, she might've found more than she bargained for."

The weight of his words settled over me like a heavy quilt. "Thank you, Horatio," I said quietly. "I appreciate your honesty."

He nodded once, his focus already shifting back to the cherries. As I turned to leave, his voice stopped me.

"Be careful, Miss," he said, his tone serious. "The past has a way of pulling people under. Don't let it take you with it."

I glanced back at him, his silhouette framed by the warm glow of the kitchen. "I'll do my best," I promised.

As I left the kitchen, I couldn't shake the feeling that Horatio had given me more than he intended. The mention of a visitor, the warning about digging too deep—it all pointed to a truth Beatrice had been desperate to uncover. And if I wasn't careful, it might lead me down the same dangerous path.

**

The kitchen door swung shut behind me, and the hallway was quieter than it had been in hours. I let the photograph weigh in my palm for a moment longer before tucking it securely into my pocket. Horatio's words echoed in my mind, and though he hadn't given me concrete answers, the weight of his warnings made it clear: Beatrice had been chasing a truth someone desperately wanted to keep hidden.

I made my way back to the sitting room, where Nick and Wiggles were chatting over a tray of mince pies Gilbert had left behind. The scent of the buttery crusts and spiced filling hung in the air, mingling with the faint, earthy aroma of the evergreen garlands lining the walls. The warm glow of the fire reflected off the antique silver tray, casting a golden light across the polished wood floor.

Nick looked up as I entered, his expression softening. "You were gone a while. Everything all right?"

I hesitated before answering, my fingers brushing over

the edge of the photograph in my pocket. "I spoke with Horatio."

Wiggles raised an eyebrow, his cup of cider halfway to his lips. "That old elf's still in service? Loyal as a bloodhound, that one. What did he have to say?"

"He wouldn't confirm much," I admitted, moving to sit beside Nick on the overstuffed sofa. "But he did hint at something. He mentioned that Mrs Harper had a visitor once, years ago, when Mr. Harper was away on business. He didn't say who the man was, but... it sounds like someone Beatrice might have learned about."

Nick frowned, leaning forward. "And you think this man could be the one in the photo?"

"It seems likely," I said, pulling the photograph from my pocket and holding it out to Wiggles. "Look at the date. Two weeks after Mrs Harper passed. That can't be a coincidence."

Wiggles set his cider down and took the photograph, his face scrunching in thought as he examined it. "Hmm. He does look uneasy, doesn't he? Like he's been cornered."

"Exactly," I said. "Horatio described Beatrice as... persistent. Maybe she pushed him to admit something. Something about her mother—or her family—that he didn't want to reveal."

Nick reached for the photograph, studying it closely. "It could be anything. An affair, financial troubles, a secret inheritance. But the date stands out. Two weeks after her mother's death? That timing seems almost sinister."

Wiggles nodded, tapping the edge of the photograph against the armrest. "And if this man was the key to whatever Beatrice was uncovering..."

"Then it makes sense why someone would want to keep him quiet," I finished softly.

Nick's hand found mine, his thumb brushing against my knuckles. "Do you think he could still be alive? This man?"

"I hope so," I said. "But if he's not... we might have to rely on what he left behind. Records, letters—anything that ties him to this family."

The grandfather clock chimed softly in the corner, and I realised how late it had grown. The house was quieter now, the bustle of the kitchen fading into a low hum. Outside the frosted windows, the snow continued to fall, blanketing the grounds in a pristine layer of white. The world felt suspended, as though the Hall itself were holding its breath, waiting for the secrets buried within its walls to be unearthed.

"I think we should start in the attic," I said finally, breaking the silence. "Horatio mentioned roots—family roots. If this man was connected to Mrs Harper, there might be something up there that ties him to her. Old letters, photographs, even a diary."

Nick nodded, his expression resolute. "I'll go with you."

Wiggles straightened, his eyes twinkling with a mix of curiosity and determination. "And I'll start asking a few questions of my own. Discreetly, of course. If there's anyone still around who remembers this man, it'll be one of the staff. People like Horatio don't forget faces, even after all these years."

I smiled faintly. "Thank you, Wiggles. Just... be careful. We don't know who we can trust yet."

He gave me a mock salute, the corners of his mouth lifting in a wry grin. "Careful is my middle name. Well, that and Candy Cane."

Nick chuckled as Wiggles stood, the photograph tucked carefully into his pocket. "I'll report back as soon as I've got something," he said, before heading toward the kitchen.

As the door swung shut behind him, Nick turned to me, his brow furrowing. "You know, you don't have to do this. The wedding, the investigation—it's a lot."

I leaned into him, resting my head on his shoulder. "I know. But I can't let this go, Nick. Beatrice deserves better than to be remembered as just another victim. And if there's a chance I can find the truth, I have to try."

He wrapped his arm around me, his warmth a comforting shield against the chill creeping into my thoughts. "Just promise me you won't take any risks. I'd like to make it to the altar with my fiancée intact."

I laughed softly, tilting my face up to kiss his cheek. "Deal. But you'd better not let me catch you playing hero either."

He grinned, his blue eyes twinkling with mischief. "I make no promises."

The fire crackled softly as we sat together, the weight of the mystery pressing down on us even in this quiet moment. The photograph lay between us on the coffee table, its creases catching the flickering light like scars. Somewhere in this house, the answers were waiting—hidden among the shadows, tucked away in forgotten corners. And though the road ahead was uncertain, I knew one thing for sure: I wasn't going to stop until I uncovered the truth.

8

———

The sitting room at Claus Cottage was aglow with the warmth of Christmas. Twinkling fairy lights framed the windows, and the soft crackle of the fire in the hearth added to the cozy atmosphere. Outside, snow drifted lazily from the sky, blanketing the world in pristine white. Inside, the air smelled of cinnamon, nutmeg, and the faint tang of pine from the garlands draped across the mantel.

I stood in the centre of it all, the star of what felt like a festive production. My arms were lifted as Lancelot DeVere, Candy Cane Hollow's most flamboyant and exacting dress designer, flitted around me like a very fashionable hummingbird. His emerald-green blazer sparkled under the glow of the lights, almost as dazzling as the dramatic sighs escaping his lips.

"Darling!" Lancelot exclaimed, holding a delicate fold of my dress aloft as though he'd unearthed a relic. "Do you see this hem? No, of course you don't. But I see it! And it is ever so slightly... off. And we simply cannot have 'off.' Not for *this* wedding."

I smiled as I thought of Nick, who had been unceremoniously banished to the study under strict orders not to catch even a glimpse of the dress. "I don't think he'll notice," I said gently. "Nick's not the kind of guy who'd spot an uneven hem."

"Nick won't notice," Lancelot replied, his tone dripping with mock horror. "But *I* will. And if I notice, it might as well be a scandal in the making. No, no, no, Holly. Perfection or nothing."

I bit back a smile as he dove to his knees, wielding a pin cushion like a weapon of great importance. Behind him, his assistants bustled about, adjusting swathes of fabric and making notes on tiny clipboards. The room was a hive of activity, yet Lancelot somehow commanded the centre of it all, a whirlwind of glitter and precision.

"Now, darling," he said, standing up to inspect his work, "take three steps forward, nice and slow. I must see how this hem behaves when in motion."

I stepped carefully down from the small pedestal his assistants had brought in, the dress moving like liquid snow around me. The fabric shimmered in the soft light, whispering against the floor with every step. For a moment, I forgot about the murder, the questions, the tension swirling in the background of my life. I felt like a bride—like the bride I'd always dreamed of being.

"Exquisite," Lancelot breathed, pressing a hand to his heart. "Absolutely exquisite. Holly, my dear, you are a vision of winter elegance. Snowflake embroidery, cascading layers —it's divine."

"Divine is one way to describe it," Nick called from the other room, his voice full of teasing affection. "Can I come back now, or am I still banished?"

"You are most certainly still banished!" Lancelot

shrieked, spinning toward the doorway as though Nick might appear at any moment. "Do you have *any* idea how bad luck it is for the groom to see the dress before the wedding?"

"Pretty sure bad luck would be me tripping over a wonky hem," Nick retorted, laughing.

I shook my head, suppressing a smile. "He's joking, Lancelot. Don't let him rile you up."

"Joking about hems," Lancelot muttered, shaking his head as he fussed with the lace train. "Honestly. The nerve."

As the room settled into a comfortable rhythm again, the soft strains of a familiar tune began to play from the record player in the corner. The harmonies of Siren Call's *Under the Mistletoe* filled the room, and I couldn't help but smile. It had been years since I'd heard this song, but it still carried me straight back to my teenage years.

"Oh, *this* song," Lancelot sighed dramatically, pressing a hand to his chest. "Siren Call was *everything*. Jason Kennedy had the voice of an angel."

"And the face of one," I added with a laugh. "Every girl in my school had his poster on her wall."

"I'll have you know I still do," Lancelot said, winking at me through the mirror. "Framed, no less. It's in my studio for daily inspiration."

"Framed?" I asked, laughing. "You're that big of a fan?"

"Jason Kennedy was an icon!" Lancelot declared, his voice full of reverence. "His voice, his hair, his... aura. Gone far too soon."

"It really was sad," I said, my voice softening. "I remember hearing about his death. It was so sudden."

Lancelot leaned closer, lowering his voice as though sharing a secret. "And suspicious. I've always thought there was more to it than the media let on. The details didn't add up."

"What do you mean?" I asked, curious despite myself.

"Just little things," he said with a dismissive wave, though his tone was anything but casual. "You hear whispers in the industry. Fashion, music—it's all connected, darling. And Jason's story never sat right with me. Such a loss."

I filed that away, my mind briefly wandering to the mysteries I might tackle after the wedding. But for now, my focus was on the here and now—on the magic of this moment.

"Now," Lancelot said, his mood brightening again as he adjusted my veil, "let us perfect the flutter. Holly, my dear, give us a little spin."

I twirled carefully, the train and veil trailing behind me like soft clouds of snow. Lancelot beamed, clapping his hands together. "Perfect! Divine! You, my dear, are the very embodiment of a winter bride."

Just then, the door creaked open, and the familiar figure of Father Christmas stepped into the room. His boots carried a fine dusting of snow that scattered across the rug as he paused in the doorway. His bright blue eyes sparkled beneath his bushy white brows, and his cheeks were rosy from the cold. But as his gaze settled on me, his usually jovial expression softened into something deeper—almost reverent.

"Holly," he said softly, his voice carrying a mix of wonder and warmth. "You look... you look radiant."

A lump formed in my throat at his words, and I found myself standing a little straighter. "Thank you," I managed, my voice quieter than I intended.

He stepped into the room, his bare socked feet looking

naked since he was so often in his big, black boots, and approached slowly, as though he were afraid to break the spell. For a moment, I was acutely aware of the swish of the dress as I shifted, the weight of the veil on my shoulders, and the faint, reassuring crackle of the fire in the background. It all seemed to fade as Father Christmas stopped a step away, his broad frame towering above me, yet his presence as gentle as the falling snow outside.

With hands that were surprisingly delicate for a man his size, he reached out and adjusted the edge of my veil where it had slipped slightly over my shoulder. His fingers trembled ever so slightly as he smoothed the fabric, and when he spoke again, his voice was thick with emotion.

"I always knew Nick would choose someone special," he said, his words measured, as though each carried the weight of generations of wisdom. "But seeing you now... I couldn't be prouder to welcome you into our family."

I swallowed hard, my heart swelling with gratitude and something else— for there was something almost paternal in the way he looked at me. "That means the world to me," I said, meeting his gaze. "I feel so lucky to be part of this family."

He chuckled softly, the sound deep and comforting, like a familiar carol sung on a snowy evening. "You're not just joining a family, Holly. You're stepping into a legacy—a life filled with joy, magic, and a little bit of chaos. But I know you'll bring a light to it that we didn't even know we needed."

The sincerity in his voice brought tears to my eyes, and I blinked quickly to keep them at bay. "I hope I can live up to it," I said, my voice barely above a whisper.

Father Christmas's smile deepened, and he placed a

large, reassuring hand on my shoulder. "You already have, my dear. Just by being who you are."

Behind him, Lancelot sniffled audibly, dabbing at his eyes with a silk handkerchief. "Oh, this is too much!" he exclaimed, his voice quivering with emotion. "I'm going to ruin my mascara. Someone bring me a mirror!"

The moment was lightened by his theatrics, and I couldn't help but laugh softly, even as my chest felt heavy with gratitude. Father Christmas stepped back slightly, taking in the full view of me in the dress. His expression was one of quiet pride, the kind that made you feel both seen and cherished.

"You're going to make a beautiful bride," he said, his voice a little steadier now. "And an even more beautiful addition to the Claus family."

"Thank you," I said again, my heart full. "That means so much."

He nodded, his eyes lingering on me for a moment longer before turning to Lancelot. "You've done a remarkable job, Lancelot. Truly. This dress—it's perfect."

Lancelot preened at the compliment, clasping his hands dramatically. "Why, thank you, Santa—I mean, Mr. Claus! Perfection is my only standard, of course. But with a bride like Holly, my work was a tad easier I'll admit."

Father Christmas chuckled, the sound warm and full of genuine affection. He turned back to me, his gaze softening once more. "I should let you finish here. But, Holly... I just want you to know how proud I am of Nick. And how grateful I am for you. You've brought something into his life—into all of our lives—that I'll never be able to thank you enough for."

I felt my cheeks warm under his kind words, but before I could respond, he gave my shoulder a final pat and stepped back toward the door. As he left, the soft creak of the hinges and the whisper of snow-dusted wind followed him, leaving behind a warmth that lingered in the room.

Lancelot let out a dreamy sigh as the door clicked shut. "Well, if that wasn't the most charming father-in-law moment I've ever witnessed. Holly, darling, you've hit the jackpot with that one."

I smiled, glancing at my reflection in the mirror. For the first time, I truly felt like a bride. The weight of the investigation, the questions swirling in the background—all of it seemed to fade, leaving only the joy of the moment and the promise of the future.

And for now, that was enough.

**

The morning at Claus Cottage started with Gilbert in full force, his energy as unrelenting as a winter blizzard. I sat at the kitchen table, a steaming mug of coffee in one hand, and a grapefruit—meticulously sliced and served by Gilbert —glaring up at me from the other.

"Eat up, darling!" Gilbert chirped, bustling around the kitchen with the kind of cheer and energy that made me tired just to watch. "You need your energy for all this sleuthing nonsense you insist on doing when you should be focused on nothing but your upcoming nuptials."

I eyed the grapefruit dubiously. "I'm not sure a grapefruit is going to help me crack the case, Gilbert."

"Nonsense!" he exclaimed, wagging a spoon at me. "Vitamin C is essential, and don't think I haven't noticed you've been skipping meals lately. A bride-to-be must glow, Holly, not merely survive. Now, eat up before I feed you myself."

I sighed and took a begrudging bite, the tartness making my lips pucker. Across the room, August leaned against the counter, scrolling through something on her tablet.

"Holly," she said without looking up, "I'll have the final wedding invitation design ready for you to check later today. Keep an eye on your phone, okay?"

I nodded, finishing off the grapefruit as quickly as I could without Gilbert noticing. "Got it. And thanks, August."

She gave me a warm smile. "No problem. Now go solve your mystery or whatever it is you're doing. But don't be late for dinner—Mrs Claus has been planning the menu all week, and she'll be heartbroken if you're not here."

"Noted," I said, grabbing my coat and scarf. Gilbert followed me to the door, handing me a travel mug filled with hot tea.

"For the road," he said, patting my arm fondly. "And do try not to get into too much trouble."

"No promises," I replied with a grin before stepping out into the crisp morning air.

By the time I reached The Olde Jolly Hall, the snow had stopped falling, leaving the grounds coated in a thick, glittering blanket of white. The Hall loomed ahead, its grand facade softened by the festive decorations adorning every window and doorway. I parked in the gravel drive and hurried inside, eager to escape the chill.

Paula was waiting for me in the foyer, clipboard in hand as always. She looked up and gave me a warm smile. "Morning, Holly. You're here early."

"I've got some... things to look into," I said vaguely, not wanting to dive into the specifics just yet. "But first, I was hoping you could help me find the attic."

Paula raised an eyebrow. "The attic? What on earth do you want to go up there for?"

"It's a long story," I admitted. "But I think it might have some of the answers I'm looking for."

She studied me for a moment before nodding. "All right. I'll take you up there. But fair warning—it's a bit of a mess. No one's done a proper clear-out in decades."

As Paula led me through the Hall, I couldn't help but notice how quiet it was. The usual hum of activity seemed muted, the festive atmosphere weighed down by the shadow of Beatrice's death. We passed the grand staircase, its banister wrapped in twinkling lights and evergreen garlands, and headed toward a narrow door tucked away in a corner of the west wing.

Charles emerged from a side corridor just as we reached the door. He looked as impeccable as ever, his suit perfectly tailored, but there was a tension in his jaw that hadn't been there the last time we'd spoken.

"Miss Wood," he said, inclining his head. "Back again?"

"Just tying up a few loose ends," I said lightly. "Paula's helping me find the attic."

His brow furrowed. "The attic? What could you possibly need up there?"

"Nothing, most likely," I replied. "But it doesn't hurt to check."

Charles hesitated, his gaze flicking to Paula before settling back on me. "Be careful up there. The floorboards are old, and some of them aren't as sturdy as they look."

"Noted," I said, surprised by his concern for my welfare. I offered him a polite smile. He didn't return it, turning instead to Paula.

"Make sure she doesn't disturb anything important," he said curtly before walking away.

"Well," Paula said, rolling her eyes as soon as Charles was out of earshot, "he's in a mood this morning."

"I noticed," I said dryly. "Is he always like that?"

"Pretty much," Paula replied with a wry smile. "But don't let him get to you. Come on, the attic's this way."

She opened the narrow door, revealing a steep staircase that spiralled upward into the dim recesses of the house. The air grew cooler as we ascended, and the faint scent of mothballs and old wood filled my nose. By the time we reached the top, my legs were burning, and I was grateful for Paula's flashlight, which illuminated the shadowy space ahead.

The attic was exactly as Paula had described: a sprawling maze of boxes, trunks, and forgotten furniture, all covered in a thick layer of dust. The ceiling sloped sharply, beams criss-crossing above us, and the single small window let in just enough light to cast long shadows across the floor.

"Here we are," Paula said, gesturing around us. "Good luck finding anything useful in this mess."

"Thanks, Paula," I said. "I'll let you know if I need anything."

The attic was vast and dimly lit, its air heavy with the scent of age and forgotten memories. Dust motes floated in the single shaft of light coming from a narrow, grime-covered window. As I scanned the piles of boxes and trunks that sprawled before me, I felt both overwhelmed and intrigued. There was a sense of history here, woven into every cobweb and creaking floorboard.

My attention was drawn to a trio of identical cardboard boxes stacked neatly against the far wall, each labelled with a Harper child's name: *Evelyn's Keepsakes, Charles' Keepsakes,* and *Beatrice's Keepsakes.* They stood out against the chaos of the rest of the attic, their labels written in the same elegant script I'd come to associate with Beatrice. It was curious that Beatrice had labelled the boxes, rather than her parents.

Did that suggest that these boxes at least had been organised recently?

I crouched in front of the stack, curiosity pulling me closer. I started with Evelyn's box, lifting the lid carefully. Inside, I found an assortment of childhood treasures that tugged at my heart. There was a well-loved teddy bear with matted fur and a missing button eye, a collection of pastel-coloured hair ribbons, and a diary bound in pink leather, its lock broken and its pages slightly yellowed. A faint scent of lavender wafted from the box, reminding me of a child's dresser filled with sachets to keep the moths away.

Next, I turned to Charles' box. It was heavier, the contents a bit more structured. On top lay a wooden train set, its tracks meticulously packed away in their original packaging. Beneath it, I found a set of marbles that glinted in the dim light, along with a small, battered trophy for a school cricket match. At the very bottom was a faded poster of a football team, its edges curling and its surface covered in faint pencil marks where a younger Charles had doodled tactics and scores.

Finally, I opened Beatrice's box. Her keepsakes felt more curated, more deliberate. There was a pristine porcelain doll with golden curls, its dress embroidered with tiny roses, and a collection of neatly bundled letters tied with a ribbon. A silver locket lay nestled among the items, its clasp slightly tarnished but still gleaming with an elegant beauty. As I held it up to the light, I wondered how many of these items Beatrice had placed here herself, and how many had been packed away by someone else after her death.

Each box told a story, a window into the lives of the Harper siblings as children. The nostalgia they evoked was bittersweet, but none of them held the answers I sought.

I sighed and set the lid back on Beatrice's box, then

turned my attention to the rest of the attic. The cluttered chaos felt overwhelming now, the sheer number of boxes and trunks making it impossible to know where to look next.

My thoughts were interrupted by the buzz of my phone in my pocket. I pulled it out, secretly pleased to have a distraction.

"Hey, sis," I said.

"Gosh, you don't sound as happy as you should this close to your wedding. Has something else happened?"

I let out a small laugh. "No, I'm just in the Harper attic, surrounded by cobwebs and probably spiders too, although I'm trying not to think of that."

"Find anything?"

"A keepsake box for each of the Harper siblings. Beyond that, the place is chaos. This isn't going to be quick. Anyway, how are things going there?" I could hear my nephew, Jeb, chat away in the background. He was accumulating new words quickly now and never tired of using them, which was wonderful because I never tired of hearing him.

"I just wanted to check you have signal because I'm going to email the wedding invitation for you to check."

"That was quick!" I exclaimed.

"I know. I was using all of these fancy fonts and none of them were right, and this morning it just came to me, keep it simple. Sometimes the right thing is hidden in plain sight. I'll send it now."

Jeb's chat gave way to the dramatic wail that I knew meant he wanted his mummy's attention back. "Oh, dear, someone isn't happy."

"Come on, Mr! We're chatting to Auntie Holly, yes we are. Okay, okay, we've done that for long enough, have we?"

August gave an indulgent laugh. She was a wonderful mother.

"You go, give him a big kiss from me," I said.

"Sorry, sis. Mummy duty calls! I'll send the design across now, okay?"

I agreed that that would be fine and ended the call. By the time I had logged into my email account, the message from August was already there. She was a whiz with anything visual, so I wasn't surprised to love her design. I sent a quick reply, in enthusiastic all capitals, saying how amazing it was and how amazing she was, and then reluctantly returned my attention to the attic.

"If I were hiding something," I muttered to myself, "where would I put it?"

The thought brought me up short. Hiding something. Not just storing it, but deliberately placing it somewhere no one would think to look. Somewhere that wouldn't attract attention. In plain sight!

I scanned the attic again, this time looking for something plain, something so ordinary it would blend into the background. My gaze landed on a small, nondescript box tucked beneath a larger pile. Its label read simply, *Accounts 2005.*

A smile tugged at my lips. If I were hiding something, this is exactly the kind of place I'd choose. I pulled the box free, brushing off the layer of dust that coated the top. The lid came off easily, revealing a stack of old receipts and ledger pages. My heart sank for a moment—had I been wrong? But as I shifted the papers aside, something caught my eye.

Nestled at the bottom of the box, wrapped in tissue paper, was a doll. My breath hitched as I carefully lifted it out. Its porcelain face was delicately painted, and its dress was adorned with intricate embroidery that could only have been done by hand. The tag hanging from its arm read *Budapest, Hungary.*

I turned the doll over, examining it for any other clues, and noticed a small envelope tucked into the folds of its skirt. My hands trembled as I opened it, revealing a neatly folded note written in elegant script.

To my dear Evelyn,

I hope this doll brings you as much joy as the thought of you has brought me. Always know that you are loved.

Dániel Lukács

The name sent a shiver down my spine. Dániel Lukács. The Hungarian doll, hidden in a box labelled for something as dull as accounts, told a story no one wanted to tell. Who was Dániel Lukács? And why had this doll been hidden away?

I stared at the note for a long moment, the pieces of the mystery swirling in my mind. This wasn't just a childhood keepsake tucked away with others—it was something more. Something someone wanted to keep buried.

As I replaced the doll and its note back in the box, my thoughts churned. The attic suddenly felt colder, the quiet pressing in around me like a weight. Whoever Dániel Lukács was, he wasn't just a figure from the past. He was a thread in the fabric of the Harper family's secrets, and I had a feeling pulling on it would unravel far more than I could imagine.

I felt almost guilty for removing the doll from her hiding place, but something compelled me to carry her with me. Whatever she had been part of, it was time she saw the light of day again.

9

———

A collective groan rippled from the kitchen as I descended the staircase at The Olde Jolly Hall, fresh from my exploration of the attic. The sound, like a chorus of exasperation, had a familiar ring to it. I paused on the final step, straining to listen. Sure enough, Gilbert's unmistakable voice rang out, high-pitched and brimming with theatrical frustration.

"Absolutely *not*! This is not a gala, this is a wedding! Do you hear me, Marcus? A *wedding!* One does not serve vol-au-vents at such an occasion without an accompanying note of whimsy!"

I bit back a laugh and hurried into the dining room, where Paula stood near the sideboard, shaking her head in amusement. She turned toward me as I approached, her expression somewhere between sympathy and disbelief. "Gilbert's back," she said simply, gesturing toward the open doorway leading to the kitchen.

"What's he upset about this time?" I asked, trying to suppress a grin.

"Apparently, the canapés lack 'soul,'" Paula replied dryly. "The kitchen staff are ready to revolt."

Another wail of indignation echoed through the hall. "And don't think I didn't notice that someone skimped on the truffle oil! Skimped! As if I wouldn't *taste* the difference!"

"I think he's adding some flavour of his own," I quipped, earning a chuckle from Paula.

Just then, Gilbert swept into the room, his scarf fluttering behind him like a superhero's cape. His expression was one of sheer exasperation, clipboard clutched tightly in his hand. "Holly!" he exclaimed, spotting me instantly. "Finally, a bride who understands the importance of culinary excellence. Perhaps you can talk some sense into these—these *try-hards!*"

Paula arched an eyebrow. "Try-hards?"

"Yes, try-hards," Gilbert said, waving his clipboard dramatically. "It's an A for effort, but a C- for achievement, I'm afraid. Do you know what they've done? They've replaced the crab cakes with... wait for it... mini fish pies. Fish pies! Are we hosting a village fair?"

"Gilbert," I began, trying to keep my tone gentle, "I'm sure whatever they're making will be delicious. The kitchen team is amazing."

"They're adequate as long as I supervise them very closely," Gilbert huffed. "But adequate isn't enough for this wedding. Holly, darling, we must rise above adequacy. We must *dazzle.*"

"Then perhaps you should dazzle the kitchen staff with some gratitude," Paula interjected smoothly. "They've been working nonstop to meet your endless demands."

Gilbert placed a hand over his heart, feigning injury. "My demands are not endless, Paula. They are precise. There's a difference."

"Sure there is," Paula muttered under her breath.

I stifled a laugh and placed a reassuring hand on Gilbert's arm. "How about you let them work their magic for now? I'm sure the menu will be perfect."

Gilbert sighed dramatically, his shoulders slumping. "Fine. I'll give them another chance. But if I find so much as a hair out of place on those petits fours, I may as well just hang up my apron for good because my name will be..."

"They'll be flawless," Paula said firmly, steering him back toward the kitchen. "And so will you, if you stop hovering."

As Gilbert disappeared into the kitchen, Paula turned back to me with a rueful smile. "Poor Marcus. He's the head chef, but when Gilbert's here, he might as well be an apprentice."

"Maybe we should warn the staff when Gilbert's on his way," I joked.

Paula chuckled. "I think they'd appreciate that. They might even bolt the door. Although, who knows, maybe the doors will be bolted soon enough, anyway."

"What do you mean?" I asked.

"Oh, ignore me. I'm just being silly," Paula said with a bat of her hand.

"Of course you're not. What's on your mind, Paula?"

She let out a long sigh. "I've been here nearly my whole life, did you know that? Seen this place through weddings, storms, and everything in between. Babies born and old folks buried. But now? What happens to the place - to the people! - after all this?"

We stood in silence for a few moments as I realised there was nothing I could say to comfort her.

"Oh, I must be going soft. Old Mrs Harper would laugh

if she saw it. She always said I was practical down to my boots."

She laughed at the memory more than was needed, and I joined in. If she'd rather gloss over her moment of high emotion, I was happy to let her. Once our laughter faded, she rubbed her hands together, clearly uncomfortable, and I decided to help her shift back into her more practical mode. I reached into my bag to pull out the doll I'd found in the attic. The morning's excitement with Gilbert had momentarily pushed it from my mind, but now the mystery felt as pressing as ever. I held up the doll for Paula to see.

"This is what I found," I said, turning it so the intricate embroidery caught the light.

Paula's expression shifted to one of curiosity. She stepped closer, her brow furrowed. "That's beautiful," she murmured. "Hungarian, isn't it? But... it doesn't seem like something the Harpers would have. It certainly wasn't the missus' taste."

"That's what I thought too," I said. "Have the family ever been to Hungary?"

"Not that I'm aware of," Paula replied, her tone thoughtful. "The old Mr and Mrs Harper adored France, and Charles is more of an Italy man. Evelyn's never mentioned any travels outside the usual tourist spots. Hungary seems a bit too obscure."

I nodded, turning the doll over in my hands. "I also found keepsake boxes in the attic—one for each of the Harper siblings. They were filled with toys and awards from their childhoods. But this doll wasn't in any of them. It was hidden."

Paula's brow furrowed deeper. "Keepsake boxes," she repeated, her voice quiet. "Of course. That attic is a mess, though, as you've seen. I'm sure all kinds of things have ended up in the wrong place up there."

"Do you think it could have belonged to someone outside the family?" I asked, holding the doll up again. "Maybe someone who gave it to them as a gift?"

I knew, from the tag, that the doll was indeed a gift, but I didn't want to reveal that information without getting Paula's thoughts. I didn't want to lead her thoughts in a particular direction.

"Possibly," Paula said, though her tone was uncertain. "But who? And why hide it?"

Before we could speculate further, Wiggles appeared in the doorway, his expression unusually serious. He gestured for us to follow him, and we trailed after him into a small office just off the main hallway. Inside, a woman in a forensic uniform was packing up her equipment with careful precision. The room smelled faintly of antiseptic, a sharp contrast to the warmth of the Hall.

Wiggles closed the door behind us and cleared his throat. "The forensic pathologist has finished her preliminary findings," he said, his voice low and steady. "Beatrice's death wasn't an accident."

A chill ran down my spine. There was no satisfaction in having my suspicions confirmed. "What was it?"

"Blunt force trauma to the head," Wiggles said grimly. "The injury wasn't consistent with a fall. She was struck with a heavy object."

Paula's hand flew to her mouth. "You're saying someone... killed her?"

"Yes," Wiggles confirmed. "And based on the state of the body, we believe she's been dead for at least six weeks."

"Six weeks?" I repeated, the timeline clicking into place. "But that means—"

"Someone was pretending to be her," Paula finished, her voice trembling. "We were getting emails, instructions... someone was impersonating her."

Wiggles nodded. "That's our working theory. We're tracking the digital correspondence now, but whoever's behind this knew how to cover their tracks."

I looked at the doll in my hands, its bright colours suddenly feeling out of place in the sterile office. "If Beatrice was keeping secrets, this might be part of it," I said, holding it out.

Wiggles took it, his expression thoughtful. "Where did you find this?"

"In the attic," I explained. "It was hidden in a box labelled 'Accounts 2005.' It seems out of place, but it might be connected."

Paula stepped closer, her voice tentative. "Do you think it has anything to do with... Evelyn?"

"Why would you think that?" I asked.

"Well, that's the year she was born."

"Do we know who this Dániel fellow is?" Wiggles asked, raising an eyebrow as he inspected the note.

"Dániel?" Paula asked, a quiver to her voice.

"That name mean something to you?" Wiggles asked.

Paula tucked a strand of hair behind her ear. "It's a blast from the past, that's for sure. I haven't thought about him in years."

"Who was he?" I asked.

"A gentleman caller of Mrs Harper's. This is many years ago, 2005 could be right although I'd have said even longer ago than that. I seem to remember speaking to him about the awful attacks of 9/11, and wasn't that before then?"

"That was 2001," I said. I remembered those horrid terrorist attacks as well. I had been walking home when a neighbour on my street opened an upstairs window to call down to me and ask me if I had heard what had happened. In some ways, my desire to become a medic had been born that day, when I had wished more than anything that I could do something to help.

"He was here often?" Wiggles asked Paula.

She cocked her head. "A few times. Mrs Harper entertained lots of people, especially back then. She became less social as she got older, like a lot of us do. But back then she was in her prime. Oh, she was beautiful, and so elegant. A fabulous host. She'd throw the most incredible balls and dinner parties. The staff would fight over who got to work those nights, it was so exciting to just be part of them."

"And Mr Harper?" I enquired.

"He was away working a lot."

"But not to Hungary?"

Paula shook her head. "Oh, no. He was in London mainly. Edinburgh sometimes, and an occasional trip to New York for conferences."

"So Mrs Harper threw parties and things to keep busy while he was away?" I asked.

"It suited them both. Mr Harper was less social, even when he was here."

"What do you remember of this Dániel fellow, then?"

"Not an awful lot. There were so many people coming in and out back in those days, you understand. I probably can't remember most of them at all. But Dániel - gosh! It's him! He's the man in the photo you showed me, isn't he?"

I gave a smile. "I was hoping he might be. That explains some things. You're sure?"

"Well, he's changed over the years of course, but yes, almost certainly. I'd forgot all about him until you mentioned his name. How curious that Beatrice would have a picture with him."

"That surprises you?"

Paula gave a definite nod. "She wouldn't have met him back then. The children were always in bed or with the nanny before guests arrived. There was a time when Dániel was here often, and not always as part of a get together, if you understand."

"You're saying that Mrs Harper had Dániel over on his own?"

Paula frowned. "I've said it as plainly as I'd like to. Mrs Harper was always good to me and I won't cast aspersions."

"Of course. You've been really helpful, Paula. Let me ask you one last question. Could this Dániel person be violent, do you think?"

Paula blew out a long burst of air from her mouth. "I honestly couldn't tell you. At the most, he's a man who I greeted and took his coat and hat. He never showed any murderous tendencies, if that's what you're suggesting, but then I can't say I've met anyone who ever has. Doesn't mean none of them could kill, if pushed."

"Well, thank you, Ms Adams," Wiggles examined the doll carefully, then placed it in an evidence bag. "We'll add this to the investigation," he said. "It could be a piece of the puzzle."

As I watched Wiggles carefully seal the doll away, a chill settled over me—not from the draughty hall, but from the gnawing question of what other secrets might still be buried, waiting to unravel everything the Harpers had worked so hard to hide.

I couldn't worry about that too much, however, because at that moment my phone vibrated in my pocket and I opened it to see a text message from Mrs Claus. Send in worrying all-caps, it screamed at me: URGENT!! CHECK EMAIL!!

10

———

The muffled hum of activity from the rest of The Olde Jolly Hall drifted faintly through the thick wooden door of the library as I stepped inside. The warmth of the room enveloped me immediately, a pleasant contrast to the draughty corridors. The fire in the hearth crackled softly, casting flickering shadows across the richly panelled walls. The smell of aged leather and polished mahogany filled the air, mingling with the faint, citrusy tang of the wax used to keep the shelves gleaming.

I set my phone on the small desk by the window and pulled up Mrs Claus' email. The subject line, "URGENT: Seating Chart Drama," practically shouted at me in her signature cheery tone. Clicking into it, I was greeted by a flurry of notes: *"Holly, darling! Aunt Marjorie cannot sit by the children's table—again! Last time, she ate their candy canes before they could. Also, do you agree with moving Uncle Rufus to the quieter corner? I worry he might not love the carol singalong."*

I couldn't help but laugh. Even her emails carried the warmth and energy of a Christmas morning. I opened the attached chart, scribbling quick notes to keep track of changes I wanted to discuss with her later.

A faint rustle from the other end of the library drew my attention. Turning, I spotted Evelyn standing near the window, half-hidden by the velvet drapes. She cradled a book in her hands, her fingers tracing its gilded spine. But she wasn't reading. Her gaze was fixed outside, on the snow-dusted grounds, her posture rigid and tense.

"Evelyn?" I said gently, not wanting to startle her.

She turned sharply, the book slipping slightly from her grip. She caught it, but her startled expression gave way to something more guarded. "Holly," she said, her tone neutral. "I didn't realise you were in here."

"Sorry if I interrupted," I replied, stepping closer. "I just needed a quiet spot to deal with some last-minute wedding details. This seemed like the perfect place. I can't even hear Gilbert's shrieks in here!"

"It's fine," she said, turning back to the window. "I was just... thinking."

The firelight cast a warm glow on her face, but her eyes remained distant, shadowed by something deeper. Her fingers tapped absently against the book's cover, the rhythm betraying her nervous energy.

I hesitated, but the opportunity to speak with her was too good to pass up. "Evelyn," I began carefully, "I wanted to ask you about something I found."

Her eyes darted to me, sharp and wary. "What is it?"

I reached into my bag and pulled out my phone, then scrolled to the photo I had taken of the doll from the attic, holding it up so the intricate embroidery caught the fire-light. "This. I found it hidden in a box labelled 'Accounts 2005.' I believe you were born that year?"

"I was," Evelyn said with a frown. "Are you suggesting my birth date is some kind of clue?"

"No, of course not! It's just, that, well, the doll seems... unusual."

Evelyn's face paled ever so slightly, her lips pressing into a thin line. "A doll?" she repeated, her voice rich with scorn. "Why would you show that to me?"

"It had a note attached," I said, keeping my tone light but firm. "It was a gift for you. From someone named Dániel. Does that name mean anything to you?"

Her arms crossed tightly over her chest, a defensive gesture that spoke volumes. "I don't know anyone named Dániel," she said quickly, her tone clipped.

Her reaction was so quick, so sharp, that it gave her away. My instincts hummed with certainty. "Are you sure?" I pressed gently. "He seemed close to your family—important, even."

"I said I don't know him," she snapped, her voice trembling slightly. She turned away, but the tension in her shoulders betrayed her.

I softened my approach, stepping closer. "Evelyn, if there's something you're keeping from me, it could help. Beatrice... she was digging into something. Something about Dániel."

At the mention of Beatrice, Evelyn flinched, her composure cracking. "You don't understand," she whispered, her voice barely audible over the crackle of the fire. "You don't know what you're asking."

"Then help me understand," I urged. "I'm not here to hurt you or your family. But Beatrice's death wasn't an accident. Someone wanted to keep her quiet."

Evelyn's breath hitched, and she gripped the back of a nearby chair for support. For a moment, I thought she might open up, but then she shook her head vehemently. "I don't know anything about that," she said, her voice rising. "And I don't know Dániel Lukács."

But as she spoke, she realised her mistake and froze. Her eyes darted to the photo of the doll, lingering on its tiny painted face, and for the briefest moment, her expression softened. "He..." she started, then stopped herself. "I can't talk about this."

"I didn't tell you his surname, Evelyn. You do know him," I said gently. "Please, what was his connection to your family?"

She shook her head, stepping back. "You don't understand. None of this—none of it—is what you think."

"What am I supposed to think?" I asked, my voice calm but insistent. "That Dániel wasn't just some distant acquaintance? That he mattered to your family?"

Her gaze flickered with something—guilt? Sadness?— and she looked away. "He wasn't supposed to matter," she said softly, almost to herself.

"Evelyn," I pressed, "if you know something about him —about why Beatrice would have had a connection to him —it could be important."

"I said I don't know!" she snapped, her voice cracking. She turned on her heel, heading for the door. "Just leave it alone, Holly. It's none of your business."

She flung the door open and disappeared down the hall, leaving me standing in the warm glow of the library with more questions than answers. My mind reeled, piecing together her reaction. She knew Dániel. That much was certain. But what was their connection? And why was she so determined to keep it a secret?

The soft click of heels on the polished floor pulled me from my thoughts. I turned to see Melinda entering the room, a glass of sherry in her hand. Her expression was unreadable, but her sharp eyes took in my presence with interest.

"Goodness," she said, her voice cool and light. "You seem to have a talent for finding yourself in the middle of things, don't you?"

"I suppose I do," I replied, matching her tone.

Melinda crossed the room with the poise of someone accustomed to commanding attention. She sipped her sherry, her gaze flicking to the phone still in my hand. "An unusual find," she remarked. "And yet, it seems perfectly suited to this place. So many hidden treasures."

"Some treasures are more hidden than others," I said carefully, watching her closely.

She smiled faintly, though it didn't reach her eyes. "That's the charm of The Olde Jolly Hall, isn't it? Secrets in every corner."

Her words carried a hint of amusement, but something about her presence felt calculated. I tucked the phone back into my bag, my focus sharpening. Melinda had a way of making every conversation feel like a game, and I wasn't sure what role she was playing yet.

As she turned to leave, she glanced over her shoulder, her smile lingering. "Good luck with your wedding, Holly. And your... investigations. I imagine you'll need it."

With that, she disappeared into the hall, leaving behind a trail of unanswered questions. My grip tightened on my bag as I turned back to the window, where Evelyn had stood moments earlier, trembling under the weight of her secrets.

Who was Dániel, and what was his connection to the Harper family? Whatever the answer, it was clear that the truth was a thread unraveling this family's carefully woven facade—and I was getting closer to pulling it free.

**

The small office tucked near the Hall's kitchen was warm and filled with the comforting hum of activity from the staff outside. Gilbert, Wiggles, and I were crowded around a polished oak desk cluttered with papers, ledgers, and Gilbert's teapot, which teetered precariously on the edge.

The air carried a medley of cozy scents—freshly baked mince pies from the kitchen and the floral hint of Gilbert's Earl Grey tea. Outside, snow fell softly, muffling the distant sounds of preparation for the upcoming wedding. It was the perfect scene for delving into a mystery, though the stakes were anything but quaint.

"Here it is," Wiggles said, pulling another ledger from the growing pile. His brow furrowed as he flipped through the pages. "Payments, transfers, invoices... hmm."

Gilbert leaned over the desk, his colourful scarf fluttering dangerously close to the tea in his cup. "You mean boring numbers and dull details, darling. You'll have to be more specific if you want me to feign interest."

"Not boring," Wiggles replied sharply. "Suspicious. These figures don't add up."

I moved closer, peering over Wiggles' shoulder. "What's off about them?"

Wiggles pointed to a line in the ledger. "These transfers were marked for event expenses, but look here—two payments to the same vendor on the same day for the same amount. That's not right."

Gilbert's eyebrows shot up. "Are we talking double-dipping? How very devious."

"It's not just the double payments," Wiggles continued, flipping further back in the ledger. "There are consistent discrepancies—small amounts, just enough to avoid notice unless you're looking closely."

"Who has access to these records?" I asked, my heart picking up pace.

"Beatrice, certainly. Maybe Charles? Some of the staff too. Probably Melinda and Paula." Wiggles said, his tone grim. "Melinda's the one who handled most of the Hall business. Paula focuses more on the day to day running of the Hall, and the staff."

Gilbert's eyes narrowed with dramatic flair. "So, our poised and perfect Melinda has been lining her pockets with Hall money? The plot thickens!"

"Not so fast," I cautioned. "We can't jump to conclusions. It's circumstantial at best."

"Circumstantial, schmircumstantial," Gilbert said, waving a hand. "If it quacks like a duck and embezzles like a thief, it's probably guilty."

Wiggles sighed, his patience fraying. "We need more than this. Melinda could explain these discrepancies as accounting errors or clerical mistakes. It doesn't prove anything."

I nodded, though my mind raced with possibilities. "But it does give us a direction. If Melinda was mismanaging funds, Beatrice might have uncovered it. That could be the connection."

Gilbert set his teacup down with a decisive clink. "Speaking of connections, have we considered that Melinda's penchant for drama rivals my own? What if she killed Beatrice to keep her little secret?"

"Gilbert," I said, shaking my head, "let's not convict her before we have all the facts."

"Well," he said, lifting his teacup again with a dramatic

flourish, "I reserve the right to call it like I see it. And this, darling, smells like guilt."

Before we could discuss further, the door creaked open. Evelyn stood in the doorway, her expression hesitant but determined. She clutched the edge of the doorframe as if it were the only thing anchoring her in place.

"I... I need to talk to you," she said, her voice barely above a whisper, her gaze fixed on me.

The tension in the room thickened, the air seemingly drawn out as everyone froze. Everyone, that is, except Gilbert.

"Oh, heavens!" he cried, leaping to his feet. With an exaggerated gasp, he tipped his teacup, sending its contents spilling across the desk in a cascade of fragrant tea.

The liquid pooled over the ledgers and papers, and Gilbert clutched his scarf dramatically. "Oh, butterfingers! What a disaster!"

Wiggles groaned, pulling a handkerchief from his pocket to blot the mess. "Gilbert," he muttered, "could you not?"

"Oh, hush, Wiggles," Gilbert replied, snatching a cloth from the side table. "These things happen when one is caught off guard by... by the sheer surprise of an unexpected guest!"

I shot him a look of both exasperation and amusement, quickly catching on to his ploy. The dramatic spill had successfully diffused the tension, giving Evelyn a moment to collect herself.

"Evelyn," I said gently, stepping toward her. "You want to talk?"

She nodded, stepping inside and closing the door behind her. Her hands twisted together nervously. "Yes. I...

I've been thinking about what you said earlier. About Dániel."

My breath hitched, and I glanced at Gilbert and Wiggles, both of whom were now quietly tidying the desk. "Go on," I encouraged, my tone soft.

Evelyn hesitated, her eyes darting between us. "I... I don't know if it matters," she said finally. "But Dániel... he was close to my mother. I mean, very close."

"How close?" I asked, careful not to sound accusatory.

Her gaze dropped to the floor. "He was... He was my godfather, I think. Or at least, that's what my mother told me when I was little. She said he was someone she trusted."

I exchanged a glance with Wiggles, whose brow furrowed in thought. "And you haven't seen him since?"

Evelyn shook her head. "Not since I was a child. But I remember he used to bring me little gifts. Dolls, mostly. Like the one you found."

"That's helpful," I said gently. "Do you know why Beatrice would have been interested in Dániel?"

Evelyn's eyes filled with tears, and she shook her head again, more adamantly this time. "I don't know. I don't know anything about her death, or about why she'd care about Dániel. I swear."

Gilbert, ever the master of timing, placed a comforting hand on her shoulder. "Darling, we're not accusing you of anything. But you can see how this might be important, yes?"

Evelyn sniffled, nodding. "Yes. But I just... I can't help you. I'm sorry."

She turned abruptly and left the room, her retreat as sudden as her arrival. The door clicked shut behind her, leaving the three of us in silence.

Gilbert broke it first, smoothing his scarf and sighing. "Well, that was enlightening."

"Enlightening but incomplete," Wiggles said, his tone thoughtful. "Dániel Lukács is a key part of this puzzle, but we're still missing something."

I nodded, as thoughts swirled in my head like snow flurries. Evelyn's reaction had been telling, but it raised as many questions as it answered. One thing was clear, though: the closer we got to the truth, the more the Harper family's secrets threatened to unravel.

"Let's keep digging," I said firmly. "There's more to this story, and I'm not stopping until we find it."

The three of us exchanged determined looks, the weight of the mystery pressing heavily against the cozy backdrop of The Olde Jolly Hall. Outside, the snow continued to fall, its pristine silence a stark contrast to the storm brewing within.

**

The cheerful hum of Claus Cottage greeted me as I stepped through the door, a wave of warmth wrapping around me like a favourite holiday blanket. The rich aroma of gingerbread baking in the oven mingled with the faint scent of pine from the Christmas tree in the corner of the den. Laughter spilled from the other room—Nick's hearty chuckle blending with Mrs Claus' sing-song voice and the occasional meow of Snowy, who was undoubtedly chasing a rogue jingle bell.

I paused for a moment, letting the warmth of home ease the tension that had built during my day at The Olde Jolly Hall. Setting my bag down on the bench near the door, I began unbuttoning my coat when a glint of gold on the side table caught my eye. Among the stack of mail and a red tin of peppermint candies was a thick, cream-coloured envelope. My name was scrawled across the front in elegant, flowing handwriting.

A smile tugged at my lips. Another Christmas card, perhaps. I picked it up, noting the embossed edges and the slight weight to it. "Someone splurged on stationery this year," I muttered to myself, imagining the charming holiday sentiment tucked inside.

Still clutching the envelope, I shrugged off my coat and draped it over the back of a nearby chair. My curiosity couldn't wait. I slid my finger under the flap, carefully pulling out the contents. The cheerful expectation dissolved instantly.

Inside was a broken candy cane, snapped neatly in two. My brow furrowed as I tilted the envelope, letting the fragile pieces drop into my palm. Strange. Beneath it was a single card, blank except for a short, chilling message scrawled in bold, black ink:

"Back off. Or I'll break you, just like this."

The laughter from the den seemed to grow louder, yet it felt like it was coming from miles away. My stomach tightened as I stared at the ominous note, the fragile candy cane lying like a warning in my hand. I read the words again, hoping they'd transform into something less threatening. They didn't.

A dozen thoughts swirled in my mind: Who would send this? How did they know where I lived? Were they watching me? Watching my family? My pulse quickened, and the festive cheer surrounding me suddenly felt fragile, like the illusion of safety had been shattered along with the candy cane.

"Holly, you're back!" Nick's voice carried from the den, followed by the sound of footsteps approaching. I quickly stuffed the card and candy cane back into the envelope and tucked it into my bag just as he appeared in the doorway, grinning. "Come join us! Mum's beating us all at Christmas trivia. It's embarrassing."

I forced a smile, hoping it looked more convincing than it felt. "In a minute. I just need to finish up something first."

Nick tilted his head, his playful smile fading as he studied me. "You okay?"

"Of course," I said quickly, straightening my posture. "I'll be right in."

He hesitated, but a call from Mrs Claus in the den drew his attention. With a wink and a shrug, he retreated, leaving me alone in the quiet hallway. I let out a breath I hadn't realised I was holding and pulled the envelope from my bag again.

The note felt heavier now, its meaning sinking in with each passing second. It wasn't just a threat—it was a warning. Someone wanted me to stop asking questions, stop digging into Beatrice's death. And whoever it was, they weren't afraid to escalate things.

I placed the candy cane halves back in the envelope, careful not to let the jagged edges press into my fingers. The weight of the gesture wasn't lost on me. Whoever sent this had been deliberate. Calculated. They knew exactly what message they wanted to send.

The sound of another burst of laughter from the den drew my attention, and I peeked around the corner. Mrs Claus was perched on the edge of the couch, holding a trivia card aloft as Nick groaned at yet another wrong answer. It was a picture-perfect scene of holiday joy—one I didn't want to disturb with my fears.

But the note lingered in my thoughts like a shadow. Someone out there wanted to intimidate me, to scare me into silence. And while it had certainly rattled me, it hadn't succeeded in its ultimate goal. If anything, it strengthened my resolve.

I slipped the envelope into the bottom of my bag and squared my shoulders. Whoever sent the threat underestimated me. They thought they could break me as easily as the candy cane they'd enclosed. But they were wrong.

Taking a deep breath, I stepped into the den, plastering on a smile as Mrs Claus beckoned me to join their game. "You're just in time for the final round!" she declared, waving me over.

"Perfect," I said, settling into the chair beside Nick. The warmth of the room and the love of my family eased some of the tension coiled in my chest, though my mind remained on the message. For now, I would enjoy this moment. But tomorrow, I'd dig even deeper.

Whoever had sent the note had just made one thing very clear: I was getting closer to the truth.

11

———————

The sitting room at The Olde Jolly Hall exuded its usual charm, with firelight dancing across the dark wood panelling and the scent of mulled cider lingering faintly in the air. Outside, the snow had begun to fall again, soft flakes piling silently on the windowsills. Inside, however, the warmth did little to thaw the icy tension.

Evelyn sat on the far edge of the worn velvet sofa, her shoulders rigid and her hands clasped tightly in her lap. The gold embroidery of her cardigan shimmered faintly in the firelight, but her downcast eyes betrayed no hint of the elegance she often carried. Charles stood by the fireplace, one hand gripping the mantel as he stared into the flames, his profile hard and unreadable. The tension in his stance matched the swirling thoughts in my mind.

I perched on the edge of a wingback chair, the room feeling both expansive and claustrophobic. My heart thudded as I pulled out my phone, the image of the Hungarian doll glowing faintly on the screen.

"Evelyn," I began, keeping my tone measured and calm,

"thank you for agreeing to talk. I know how difficult all of this has been."

Her eyes flicked to me, a glint of apprehension flashing through her otherwise guarded expression. "I don't know what else there is to say," she murmured, her voice brittle. "It's all been... overwhelming."

"I understand," I said softly, though the tension in the room made it clear she didn't fully believe me. "But there are still some pieces of this that don't quite fit. I think you might have some of the answers."

Charles shifted, his jaw tightening. "Evelyn has nothing to do with this," he said sharply. "She's already been through enough."

"I'm not accusing her of anything," I replied evenly. "But I need to understand. Beatrice's death wasn't random, and the more I uncover, the clearer it becomes that someone wanted to silence her."

Evelyn's head snapped up, her pale features framed by the soft glow of the firelight. "Silence her?" she repeated, her tone wavering. "You think she was killed because of a secret?"

"Yes," I said, my voice firm but gentle. "And I believe it's connected to something she discovered—something about Dániel Lukács."

The mention of his name made Evelyn flinch, her hands clenching tighter in her lap. Charles turned sharply, his gaze dark and protective. "You have no idea what you're talking about," he said, his voice low and dangerous.

"Maybe I don't," I admitted, holding my ground. "But I know what I've found. Evelyn, this doll—it was a gift to you, wasn't it? From Dániel Lukács?"

"I barely remember, I was just a child," Evelyn said

quickly, too quickly. Her gaze darted to Charles, and the unspoken plea in her eyes was impossible to miss.

I sighed softly, leaning forward to meet her gaze. "Evelyn, I'm not trying to hurt you. But I found this doll hidden in the attic, with a note from Dániel. It was meant for you. Beatrice must have known about it—about him."

"I said I don't remember," Evelyn snapped, but her voice trembled, betraying her. "I've told you all I can. Why can't you just leave it alone?"

"Because this isn't just about you," I said firmly. "Beatrice is dead. Someone killed her to protect a secret, and I need to know if that secret involves Dániel Lukács."

The silence that followed was deafening. Evelyn's lower lip trembled, her eyes darting between me and her brother. Charles pushed off the mantel, his fists clenched at his sides. "Enough," he barked. "You've got no right to interrogate her like this."

"I'm not interrogating her," I shot back, standing to face him. "I'm trying to get to the truth."

Charles stepped closer, his frame imposing. "You want the truth?" he said, his voice low and bitter. "Fine. Dániel Lukács is her father."

"Charles!" Evelyn cried, her voice breaking. She leapt to her feet, her face crumpling as tears spilled down her cheeks. "Why would you—why would you say that?"

"Because you can't keep running from it," he said, his tone softening. He placed a steadying hand on her shoulder, his expression a mix of frustration and sorrow. "You deserve to tell your story before someone else does."

Evelyn buried her face in her hands, her sobs muffled against her palms. I stood frozen, the weight of Charles' revelation settling heavily in the room. The fire popped in the hearth, the only sound as we all grappled with the truth.

Taking a deep breath, I approached Evelyn slowly, crouching slightly to meet her eye level. "Evelyn," I said softly, "I know this isn't easy. But I need to understand. What happened between your mother and Dániel?"

She sniffled, lowering her hands but avoiding my gaze. "I didn't know," she whispered, her voice barely audible. "My whole life, I thought he was just... a family friend. A godfather, Mum called him. He'd send gifts sometimes, but he never... he was never around."

"What changed?" I asked gently.

Evelyn hesitated, glancing at Charles, who nodded slightly. She took a shaky breath. "Before Mum died," she said, her voice trembling, "Beatrice found some letters. From him. Letters that Mum had kept hidden for years."

"Hidden?" I pressed, my pulse quickening.

"Beatrice was furious," Evelyn continued. "She confronted Mum, accused her of betraying the family. And then, after Mum passed... Beatrice told me. She said she'd figured it out. That Dániel wasn't just a godfather. He was my father."

My chest tightened at the raw pain in her voice. "Did you ever meet him?" I asked.

"Not that I can remember," she said, shaking her head. "I think he visited when Dad was away, but I don't really remember."

"Have you had any contact with him since your mum died, Evelyn? Please think carefully, it's an important question," I asked.

She shook her head and began to cry again. "I didn't want to. I didn't know how to feel about it. And Beatrice... she made it clear she thought I didn't belong here. I didn't want to prove her right. I didn't want to be disloyal. She said she'd make sure I didn't get a penny from the estate. That I didn't deserve it."

Charles swore under his breath, his anger simmering. "Beatrice was cruel. She wanted power, control. She would have destroyed Evelyn just to feel superior."

"But that doesn't mean I killed her!" Evelyn cried, her voice cracking. She turned to me, her tear-streaked face full of desperation. "I hated her, but I didn't kill her. I swear, Holly."

"I believe you," I said, though I wasn't at all sure that I did. "But someone did. And if Beatrice was threatening to cut you out of the estate, it could be connected."

Evelyn shook her head, fresh tears spilling down her cheeks. "I didn't do it," she whispered. "I swear."

Before I could ask more, Paula's voice called from the hall. "Miss Wood? You're needed in the study."

I glanced toward the door, then back at Evelyn and Charles. "We're not done," I said softly. "If there's more you know—about Beatrice, about Dániel—I need you to tell me."

Evelyn said nothing, her gaze fixed on the floor. Charles stepped between us, his expression hard. "That's enough for today," he said firmly. "Go to your meeting."

Reluctantly, I left the room, my mind spinning with the weight of what I'd learned. Dániel Lukács wasn't just a name in the past—he was a thread in a tapestry of secrets, and I was unraveling it one piece at a time.

**

The corridors of The Olde Jolly Hall seemed quieter now, as though the Hall itself was holding its breath. Paula and I walked side by side, her footsteps soft against the polished wood floors. Outside, snowflakes drifted lazily, settling on the frosted panes of the tall windows. Despite the cozy warmth of the Hall, a faint chill lingered in the air, as if the secrets hidden within its walls had seeped into the very fabric of the building.

"So," I began casually, adjusting my scarf as we rounded a corner, "it must cost a fortune to run this place!"

Paula laughed. "It's eye watering."

"And Beatrice kept track of it all on her own?"

Paula glanced at me, her lips pressing together in a thoughtful frown. "Goodness, no. Beatrice was thorough—some might even say obsessive—but even she couldn't juggle it all. The Hall's finances have always been… complicated."

"Complicated how?" I asked, matching her pace as we passed a gilded mirror that reflected the warm glow of sconces lining the hallway.

"Well, it's not just the usual revenue and expenses," Paula explained, her voice low. "There's the estate's maintenance, the events we host, the charity functions, not to mention the restoration projects Beatrice was so passionate about."

"Who else had access to the financial records?" I pressed gently, keeping my tone conversational.

She sighed, her breath forming a soft puff in the cool air. "The accountant, of course. Officially, they're responsible for reconciling everything. But Melinda handled most of the daily tracking—inventory, vendor payments, that sort of thing."

"What about Charles?" I asked, watching her reaction closely.

Paula nodded. "He was more involved with the larger projects. Renovations, negotiating contracts for big events. He's got an eye for detail, even if he's not the easiest person to work with."

"And you?"

Paula's laugh was soft, almost self-deprecating. "Me? I manage the basics—staff wages, ordering supplies. I never touched the larger sums. That was Beatrice's domain."

"So, pretty much everyone in the inner circle had access," I said lightly, though my thoughts were anything but.

Paula's steps faltered slightly, her gaze sharpening. "Are you suggesting something, Holly?"

"Not at all," I said quickly, offering her a reassuring smile. "It's just that the Hall's finances seem to have been a bit... contentious recently."

She nodded slowly, her expression guarded. "Beatrice started combing through everything a few months ago. She said she wanted to make sure everything was above board. I thought it was just her usual perfectionism, but... maybe she found something."

The conversation left an uneasy tension between us as we reached the door to the study. Muffled voices spilled into the corridor, the lively tones clashing with the heaviness in my chest. Paula pushed the door open, and we stepped into a scene of controlled chaos, but Paula reached for my hand, gave me a steely gaze and told me, "I can assure you, I have never taken a penny that doesn't belong to me."

Interesting. I'd never suggested she had.

The study was a hive of activity, the scent of spiced cider mingling with the faint tang of waxed wood. A roaring fire crackled in the hearth, its warmth drawing the chill from my cheeks. Gilbert stood at the head of the room, gesturing animatedly as he addressed a small gathering of staff.

"Turkey roulade," he proclaimed, his voice carrying a theatrical flair, "is not merely a dish! It's a declaration! A statement of sophistication! A crescendo of culinary brilliance! A war against substandard fare!"

A faint groan rippled through the room as Marcus, the head chef, pinched the bridge of his nose. "And here I thought it was just turkey," he muttered, earning a round of stifled laughter.

Gilbert whirled on him, clutching his clipboard dramatically. "Just turkey? *Just* turkey? Marcus, darling, you're going to give me an aneurysm with that kind of thinking. This is precisely why I'm here!"

I exchanged an amused glance with Paula as we slipped into the room. The table was strewn with papers—seating charts, sketches of centrepieces, and detailed menus scribbled with notes in Gilbert's elegant handwriting. A tray of mince pies sat nearby, their buttery scent making my stomach rumble.

"Now," Gilbert continued, turning back to the group, "let's discuss the amuse-bouche. I want sophistication, whimsy, and just a hint of nostalgia. Think winter in the French Alps—charming, but not cliché."

Marcus sighed, his arms crossed. "Gilbert, you're asking for a lot."

"And you're paid for a lot," Gilbert shot back, raising an eyebrow. "Don't tell me the head chef of The Olde Jolly Hall can't conjure a little magic."

"Why don't you conjure it yourself?" Wiggles quipped from the corner, earning another round of chuckles. He balanced a plate stacked high with mince pies on his stomach. Clearly, he had reached a lull in his investigation.

Gilbert placed a hand over his heart, feigning offence. "Why don't I conjure it myself? Why not, indeed! Trying to delegate a single, tiny job is pointless in this place, clearly!

Why, I've got a good mind to hang up my apron and be done with it all!"

The lively banter brought a welcome lightness to the room, though the undercurrent of tension lingered in the back of my mind. I joined Paula near the sideboard, where she began organising a pile of floral arrangement sketches.

"Is it always like this?" I asked, gesturing toward the spirited group.

Paula laughed softly. "When Gilbert's involved, yes. He has a way of making everything seem both urgent and absurdly theatrical."

I reached for one of the mince pies, the buttery pastry flaking perfectly as I bit into it. "Well, at least he keeps things interesting."

The door creaked open, cutting through the laughter like a sudden gust of wind. Charles stepped inside, his presence instantly shifting the mood. His face was pale, his shoulders hunched as though he were carrying an invisible weight.

"Charles?" Paula said, her voice tinged with concern. "What's wrong?"

He hesitated, his gaze flicking to me before darting around the room. "Holly," he said finally, his voice low. "I need to speak with you. Alone."

Gilbert's eyes lit up with exaggerated intrigue. "Oh, my! Drama in the study! Whatever could it be?"

"Not now, Gilbert," Paula said firmly, steering him toward the door. "Let's give them some privacy."

Gilbert muttered something about timing and intrigue as the others followed him out, leaving Charles and me alone in the suddenly too-quiet room. He sank into a chair near the fire, his hands trembling as he rubbed them together.

"What's going on, Charles?" I asked, taking the seat across from him.

He stared into the flames, his jaw tight. "I need to tell you the truth," he said, his voice barely audible. "About Beatrice."

A chill ran down my spine despite the warmth of the room. "What truth?"

Charles' hands clenched into fists, his knuckles white. "It was my fault. Her death—it's on me."

My heart pounded in my chest. "What are you saying, Charles?"

He leaned forward, his face etched with anguish. "We argued that night. About Evelyn, about Dániel. Beatrice was determined to cut Evelyn out of the estate. She said she wouldn't let a—" He stopped himself, shaking his head. "It doesn't matter what she said."

"Go on," I urged gently.

"She threatened to go public with everything," he continued, his voice cracking. "I tried to stop her. I grabbed her arm, but she pulled away and fell—into the passageway."

"The passageway?" I asked, frowning.

"It's an old staff passage," Charles explained. "Barely used anymore. Beatrice always said it was a safety hazard, but she never got around to sealing it off."

I leaned forward, my mind racing. "But the forensic report said she died from a blow to the head. That doesn't sound like a fall."

Charles flinched, his head shaking vehemently. "I didn't hit her! I swear, Holly, I didn't. But if I hadn't confronted her, she wouldn't have been there. She wouldn't have—" His voice broke, and he buried his face in his hands.

The crackle of the fire filled the silence as I processed his words. Charles' guilt was evident, but his story didn't add up. The passageway, the argument, the injury—it left more questions than answers.

"Charles," I said softly, "what aren't you telling me?"

He lifted his head, his eyes glistening. "I've told you everything I know," he whispered. "But here's more. I'm not even sorry she's dead. That's the truth of it."

The weight of his words settled over me like a heavy blanket. The truth was closer, but it remained just out of reach, cloaked in the shadows of this fractured family.

12

———————

The fire in the study crackled softly, but the tension in the room was anything but cozy. Charles sat slumped in the armchair, his face pale but resolute, his hands clenched tightly in his lap. Evelyn hovered near the door, her eyes wide and brimming with tears as she stared at her brother.

"You have to stop," Evelyn pleaded, her voice trembling. "Charles, please, stop this nonsense."

"It's not nonsense," Charles replied, his voice steady but hollow. "It's the truth."

I stood by the window, my arms crossed as I studied them both. The warm glow of the fire did little to soothe the chill creeping up my spine. Something about Charles' confession didn't sit right. His words were precise, almost rehearsed, as if he'd prepared for this moment. And Evelyn —her protests weren't just defensive. They were desperate.

"Charles," I said, keeping my voice calm, "why don't you tell me exactly what happened? Start from the beginning."

He exhaled slowly, leaning forward and resting his

elbows on his knees. "We argued that night," he began, his tone flat. "Beatrice and I were in the passageway. She was furious about... Evelyn. About everything. She said she was going to cut her out of the estate, humiliate her publicly. I couldn't let her do that."

Evelyn gasped, covering her mouth with her hand. "Charles, no! You're lying!"

"I tried to stop her," Charles continued, ignoring Evelyn's outburst. "We struggled. I... I hit her. She fell, and I panicked. I didn't mean to, but it was too late."

"Too late for what?" I pressed, narrowing my eyes. "Did you check her pulse? Did you see if she was breathing?"

Charles hesitated, his fingers twitching slightly. "I... no. I just knew. I left her there."

Evelyn let out a choked sob, stepping toward him. "You didn't kill her, Charles! You're saying this because of me, aren't you? You think I did it!"

His silence spoke volumes. Evelyn's face crumpled, and she turned to me, her voice cracking. "You have to believe me. I didn't hurt her. I didn't even know about the passageway until... until she was found."

I glanced at Charles, who refused to meet my gaze. His confession felt like a shield, an attempt to protect Evelyn from the scrutiny of an investigation. But it didn't add up. The injuries, the timeline—none of it matched his story.

"Evelyn," I said gently, "why would Charles think you're involved?"

She shook her head frantically, tears streaming down her face. "I don't know! Because Beatrice hated me? Because she thought I didn't deserve anything? But I swear, Holly, I didn't touch her."

Charles stood abruptly, his chair scraping against the

wooden floor. "That's enough," he snapped. "I told you what happened. Now do what you need to do."

Before I could respond, a rap at the door interrupted us and Wiggles stepped inside, his expression a mix of curiosity and concern. I'd texted him to say we would need him, and a pair of handcuffs. "Everything all right in here?" he asked, glancing between the three of us.

"No," Charles said immediately, his voice firm. "I need to confess. I killed Beatrice."

Wiggles raised an eyebrow, his sharp gaze flicking to me. I shook my head subtly, silently signalling my doubt. But Wiggles played along, stepping further into the room. "Why don't you explain that to me?" he said, his tone even.

Charles repeated his story, the same practiced version he'd told me. Wiggles listened patiently, his arms crossed, his expression unreadable. When Charles finished, Wiggles nodded slowly. "All right," he said. "Charles Harper, I'm placing you under arrest."

"What?" Evelyn shrieked, rushing to her brother. "You can't! He's lying! He didn't do it!"

"Evelyn," Wiggles said gently but firmly, "this is standard procedure. We'll investigate thoroughly, but right now, we need to follow protocol."

He pulled out his phone and made a quick call. Within minutes, a junior officer arrived, her expression professional but sympathetic. She escorted Charles out of the room. Evelyn followed after him, sobbing as she vowed to get him the best lawyer.

I turned to Wiggles, my jaw tight. "He's covering for someone," I said quietly. "I'm sure of it."

"Evelyn, maybe?" Wiggles suggested, his tone cautious.

"Maybe," I admitted. "But it doesn't add up. There's something else going on here."

Wiggles nodded thoughtfully. "What do you have for me?"

I pulled out the ledger and laid it on the desk, flipping to the pages marked with discrepancies. "I still think the accounts are part of it. Beatrice was combing through these records before she died. She found irregularities—double payments, strange transfers. It's embezzlement, but subtle enough to avoid detection unless you're looking for it."

Wiggles scanned the pages, his expression growing more serious. "And who had access to these records?"

"Melinda, for sure," I said. "The accountant, Paula, and Charles too."

Wiggles frowned, flipping through the ledger. "This gives us a motive, but it's not enough. Everyone here seems to have had a motive to kill Beatrice."

"You're right," I agreed. "Charles says he killed her to protect Evelyn's secret. Evelyn could have killed Beatrice for the same reason. And anyone with access to the accounts could have been stealing money, and killed Beatrice when she discovered it."

The crackle of the fire in the study provided a comforting backdrop, though it did little to ease the tension hanging in the room. Wiggles had settled into one of the chairs, the ledger spread open across his lap, while I leaned forward, elbows on my knees, studying the figures we'd been dissecting for what felt like hours.

The silence between us was heavy, punctuated only by the occasional rustle of paper as Wiggles flipped back and forth through the ledger. Finally, he sighed, leaning back in his chair and rubbing his temple.

"This," he said, tapping a column of figures with the back of his pen, "is meticulous work. The same amount, carefully duplicated. Small enough not to raise flags but steady enough to add up over time. It's deliberate."

"And it's someone who knew Beatrice wasn't watching closely until recently," I added. "If they thought they could get away with it, they'd keep doing it."

Wiggles nodded. "So, let's break this down properly. The accountant. They're the ones ultimately responsible for reconciling these books, aren't they?"

"Yes, but their job is to review, not create," I said. "They'd notice errors, not orchestrate them. And they're external—they don't have access to day-to-day transactions."

Wiggles pursed his lips, considering. "True. But if they wanted to slip something in, they could argue it was just a mistake during reconciliation."

I frowned. "Maybe. But why would they take the risk? The accountant would have the least to gain and the most to lose. Their entire reputation hinges on accuracy."

"And if Beatrice was reviewing these, she'd have gone after them immediately," Wiggles agreed. He made a note in the margin of the ledger. "All right, who's next?"

"Paula," I said, straightening. "She handles staff wages and supply orders. She's meticulous, but that's about it. She wouldn't touch the bigger expenses."

"She does have access," Wiggles pointed out. "If she wanted to, she could shift things around without anyone noticing."

I shook my head. "It doesn't fit. Paula's more about keeping things running smoothly—she thrives on order, not deception. And when I spoke to her earlier, she was adamant she hadn't taken anything. She practically swore it."

"She could be lying," Wiggles said, his tone neutral.

"People can be convincing when they've got something to hide."

"But she doesn't benefit," I countered. "Paula's been with the Hall for years. She's loyal to the family. I just can't see her risking everything. Unless..."

"Unless what?"

"She's very protective of the staff. I don't think she'd steal for her own benefit, but maybe she was helping an employee financially?"

"An altruistic thief is still a thief," Wiggles leaned back, nodding slowly. "All right. Let's move on to Charles."

I exhaled, feeling the weight of the evening pressing against me. "Charles is emotional, volatile even, but I don't think he's calculated enough for this."

"Volatile's an understatement," Wiggles muttered. "But he's in a position of power here. Contracts, major projects, renovations. If he wanted to siphon off money, he'd have plenty of opportunities."

"True," I admitted. "But he's not the one handling the daily finances. These duplicate payments? They're subtle. He doesn't strike me as someone who would—or could—be that precise."

Wiggles scratched his chin, his brow furrowed. "You might be right. He doesn't seem the type to play the long game. And he's too focused on protecting Evelyn right now."

"Exactly," I said, leaning forward. "When he confessed earlier, he didn't sound like a man trying to cover up financial crimes. He sounded like someone willing to take the fall for his sister."

Wiggles closed the ledger and rested it on his lap. "Which brings us to Melinda."

I nodded, the weight of her name settling over the room. "She's the most logical suspect. She handles the daily operations—vendor payments, event costs, supplies. She has access to everything Beatrice would've reviewed."

"And she's clever," Wiggles added. "Poised, professional, but always just a little too polished."

"It's not just her demeanour," I said, pointing to the ledger. "These discrepancies? They're small, but they show someone who knows the system inside and out. Melinda's in the perfect position to pull this off without anyone noticing."

"Until Beatrice did," Wiggles said grimly. "And if Beatrice confronted her, it would explain a lot."

"Like motive," I finished. "If Melinda had been embezzling for years and Beatrice threatened to expose her, she'd have a lot to lose."

"Her career, her reputation," Wiggles said, ticking off the points on his fingers. "And probably her freedom."

"And then there's her response earlier," I said, recalling Melinda's guarded tone when we'd spoken. "She's been deflecting, avoiding specifics. It's like she knows we're circling closer."

Wiggles leaned forward, his elbows resting on his knees. "So, we've got motive, opportunity, and behaviour that lines up. But it's still not proof."

"No," I agreed. "But it's enough to make her our prime suspect."

Wiggles let out a long breath, the firelight flickering against his weathered face. "All right. We confront her. Together."

I nodded. "Agreed. If she's behind this, we'll get to the truth."

He stood, tucking the ledger under his arm. "But no jumping to conclusions. We'll let her hang herself with her own words, if she's guilty."

"Understood," I said, standing as well. "But I have a feeling Melinda's not going to make this easy."

Wiggles gave a wry smile. "Nothing about this case has been easy, Holly. Why should this be any different? My officers even had to abandon their trip to Candy Cane Custody because of the storm that's rolling in. They've brought Charles back here to hold him under house arrest. Or, should that be Hall arrest?"

As we left the study, I noticed that the weather really had taken a turn for the worse. The snow continued to fall, but there was nothing peaceful about it anymore. Instead, the wind blew so hard it caused the old windows to rattle, and I shivered just as I looked out at it, glad to at least be inside and warm.

**

The wind howled like a wild beast outside The Olde Jolly Hall as I hurried through the corridors with Wiggles by my side. My breath was sharp in my chest, not just from the rush but from the biting cold that seeped into the Hall despite its thick stone walls. We had been searching for more than two hours and it was clear that Melinda was gone, vanished without a word, and my gut churned with a mixture of urgency and dread.

"She can't have gone far," I said, my voice a little breathless. The storm outside was worsening, and the idea of anyone wandering off into it—even someone like Melinda—felt reckless.

"She better not have," Wiggles muttered. His jaw was set in that determined way of his, and I could tell he was already piecing together contingencies in case she had managed to slip away completely.

We passed the kitchen, where the comforting scent of caramelised onions and roasting turkey mingled with the warmth of the ovens. I hesitated, pushing the door open to check if anyone had seen her. Marcus glanced up from a cutting board, where he was meticulously slicing butternut squash and beetroot into perfect cubes.

"Have you seen Melinda?" I asked, trying to keep the edge out of my voice.

Marcus frowned. "Not since earlier," he said, wiping his hands on a dish towel. "She came in muttering something incoherent and grabbed a glass of wine before leaving."

"She drank the wine?" Wiggles said, his tone sharp.

Marcus shrugged. "She seemed... distracted. I didn't think much of it. She didn't say where she was going."

My stomach twisted. Wine and distraction didn't bode well. "Thanks, Marcus," I said, already stepping back into the corridor. "Let us know if you see her."

As Wiggles and I turned a corner, my eyes caught something through the frosted window—a trail of faint marks in the snow, barely visible in the storm's fury. My heart jumped. "Wiggles," I said, grabbing his arm and pointing. "Look."

He squinted through the glass, his expression hardening. "Tracks. Fresh."

I didn't need to be told twice. Pulling my scarf tighter around my neck, I followed Wiggles to the front door. The storm hit us the moment we stepped outside, the icy wind tearing at my coat and scarf like it had a personal vendetta against them. Snowflakes swirled chaotically, and my boots sank into the deep drifts, each step a struggle.

"There!" I shouted, spotting a dark figure near the edge of the property. My heart pounded as I pointed toward the silhouette. "Is that her?"

Wiggles shielded his eyes against the flurries and nodded. "It's her. Let's move."

The snow numbed my face, the wind stealing my breath as we trudged through the storm. The figure grew clearer— a lone woman standing beside a low sports car. My pulse quickened as we approached, every nerve on edge.

"Melinda!" Wiggles bellowed, his voice cutting through the storm.

She turned slowly, her face calm and unreadable despite the chaos around her. Her coat flapped in the wind, and snow clung to her hair, but she stood with an eerie stillness.

"Chief Inspector Wiggles," she said, her voice even and controlled. "Miss Wood. What an unexpected visit."

"Melinda," I said, stepping closer despite the cold biting through my gloves. "What are you doing out here?"

She gestured toward the car, her movements unnervingly composed. "I'm on my way to Candy Cane Custody," she said, as if that were the most logical thing in the world.

"Why?" Wiggles demanded, his brow furrowing.

"To turn myself in, of course," she replied smoothly.

'To turn yourself in for what?" I asked.

Melinda raised a perfectly shaped eyebrow in amusement. "For embezzlement. Hadn't you worked it out yet? I didn't want that trivial matter to distract you from solving poor Beatrice's murder, but now that Charles is locked away where he belongs, I thought it best to handle this matter without further disruption to the family."

I stared at her, disbelief warring with suspicion. "During a blizzard?"

She chuckled as if I'd asked something foolish. "I'm born and raised in Candy Cane Hollow, unlike some people. I've seen blizzards before. Where are you two going, anyway? Do you need a lift?"

"That vehicle's entirely inappropriate for this weather, and you know it," I scolded her. It was a pet peeve of mine, people who took silly risks with their own safety and then needed the overworked emergency services to go out and rescue them.

Wiggles' jaw tightened. "You're coming back to the Hall with us," he said firmly. "We'll sort this out inside."

Melinda's lips twitched into a faint smile. "If you insist."

The walk back was brutal. The storm seemed to grow angrier with every step, the wind howling around us as snow lashed at my face. My boots slipped more than once on the icy ground, and I had to clutch Wiggles' arm to steady myself.

Inside, the Hall felt like a haven, its warmth enveloping us as we shook off the snow. I stomped my boots against the floor, shivering as the heat began to seep into my frozen limbs. Melinda, however, seemed unaffected, brushing the snow from her coat with quiet precision.

"Sit," Wiggles ordered, gesturing to a bench in the foyer. Melinda complied without protest, folding her hands neatly in her lap. Her calmness set my teeth on edge. It wasn't natural.

"What exactly do you want to confess?" I asked, my arms folded across my stomach.

Melinda looked up at me, her eyes wide and innocent. "Oh, no big deal. You'll see some things that don't quite add up in the Hall's accounts, that's all."

"And you're admitting you're responsible for them?"

Melinda laughed. "You're making it all sound very serious, Holly. If only poor Beatrice hadn't died, it wouldn't even be worth mentioning to anyone. But I know how things can look. It's so easy for two plus two to equal five sometimes."

"You were stealing from your employer." Wiggles said.

"Beatrice was my friend, not my employer. We were open books with each other. I know everything there is to know about this place, about the runnings of the great Hall. If I was a bit short, I duplicated an invoice and sent myself a little extra. Nothing dodgy!"

"It sounds dodgy," I muttered.

"It sounds like a criminal offence that will get you locked up in Candy Cane Custody. You're smart enough to know that."

"Which is exactly why I was going across to see your colleagues and explain everything, before it could look suspicious. Beatrice trusted me implicitly. It's just awful what Charles did to her. You know, she was always scared of him."

My ears cocked up at this revelation. "She was?"

Melinda nodded. "The two of them would play in that passageway and he would lock her in there. She'd scream and scream before he let her out. He's always been awful."

"How do you know that?"

"I grew up here. Didn't you know? My mum had this job before I did. Gosh, me and Beatrice were like sisters."

Before I could ask more, a sharp knock echoed through the Hall. It was deliberate, heavy, and filled with an ominous weight that froze everyone in place.

The knock came again, louder this time, reverberating through the space like a warning. My heart skipped a beat as I exchanged a glance with Wiggles. Who could it possibly be at this hour, in this storm?

"Stay here," Wiggles said quietly, his hand resting on the back of a chair as he turned toward the door. I followed, my chest tightening with anticipation.

The knock came a third time, each beat resonating with an eerie finality. Wiggles reached for the handle, pausing to glance at me. "Ready?"

I nodded, my breath hitching as the door creaked open.

Snow swirled into the foyer, the wind carrying a chill that seemed to cut straight to the bone. A shadowy figure stood on the threshold, their face obscured by the storm.

"Who's there?" Wiggles demanded, his voice sharp.

The figure stepped forward, and in the dim light, their features began to take shape. My breath caught, the truth hovering just out of reach. Whatever lay beyond that door, I knew it would change everything.

13

My fingers tightened around the edge of the side table as Wiggles reached for the door.

With a sharp pull, the door creaked open, and a flurry of snow burst inside, the icy wind biting against the warmth of the Hall. A man stood silhouetted in the storm, his heavy coat dusted with snow and his hat clutched in one gloved hand. He stepped forward, his face partially illuminated by the chandelier above. Dark hair streaked with grey framed a face drawn tight with cold and something deeper—fear.

"Where is she?" the man demanded, his voice rich with an accent that caught my attention. "Evelyn. Is she here? Is she safe?"

Wiggles held up a hand to block him from entering. "Whoa there, fella. Who exactly are you?"

"I'm Dániel Lukács," the man said, his voice trembling with urgency. "I'm her father. And I need to know—" His voice cracked, and he swallowed hard. "I need to know she's all right."

The name hit me like a jolt, confirming what I'd

suspected but hadn't fully dared to believe. This was Evelyn's father—the man at the centre of so many tangled threads in this mystery.

"She's safe," I said, stepping forward before Wiggles could block him further. "But why are you here, Dániel? And in this storm?"

His shoulders slumped slightly, the tension in his stance giving way to exhaustion. "I heard... I heard a Harper woman had been killed," he admitted, his voice thick with emotion. "I thought it might be Evelyn. I couldn't just stay away."

Wiggles narrowed his eyes, but he stepped aside. "Come in before you freeze to death. We'll get you a hot cocoa."

"I'm on it!" Gilbert called from behind us. I swear he has an innate alert for people's sugary needs.

As Dániel entered, the warmth of the Hall enveloped him, and he stamped his boots against the mat, snow melting into tiny puddles on the polished floor. He brushed the frost from his coat, revealing a worn but well-tailored suit underneath. His gaze swept the grand foyer, lingering on the ornate decorations and high-arched ceilings.

"So, I'm here again," he murmured, almost to himself. "I always knew she'd grow up surrounded by this, but..." His voice trailed off, his expression a mix of awe and regret.

"Do you care for Evelyn?" I asked softly, watching his face.

His eyes snapped to mine, dark and intense. "She's my daughter," he said simply. "Of course, I care for her. I always have."

Before I could respond, hurried footsteps echoed down the corridor, and Evelyn appeared, her golden hair tumbling loose around her pale face. She stopped short at the sight of Dániel, her eyes wide with disbelief.

"Da... Dániel?" she whispered, her voice cracking. "What... what are you doing here?"

Dániel froze, his hands tightening around his hat. For a moment, they stared at each other, the space between them charged with unspoken emotion. Then, with a sudden burst of movement, Evelyn rushed to him, throwing her arms around his neck.

He caught her, holding her tightly as though she might vanish. "Evelyn," he whispered, his voice breaking. "Thank God. I thought... I thought I'd lost you."

Tears streamed down her cheeks as she pulled back to look at him, her hands gripping his coat. "You shouldn't have come," she said, her voice thick with both relief and reproach. "It's not safe."

Dániel cupped her face gently, his thumbs brushing away her tears. "I couldn't stay away. Not when I thought you might be in danger."

"You didn't think to write?" she asked, a mix of anger and heartbreak in her tone. "To explain? After all these years, you just show up now?"

"I thought your mother would tell you," Dániel said, his voice laden with guilt. "I thought it was better this way. Safer."

Evelyn stepped back, her arms dropping to her sides. "She didn't. Beatrice did. And she hated me for it."

Dániel's brow furrowed. "Hated you? Why?"

"Because I'm not a true Harper," Evelyn said bitterly. "Because she thought I didn't belong."

Dániel's face darkened, his jaw tightening. "Beatrice always was... headstrong. But I never thought she'd—"

"She's dead," I interrupted gently, stepping closer. "She was murdered, Dániel."

His head snapped toward me, his eyes wide with shock.

"Murdered? My God... Evelyn, don't talk to these people—you need a lawyer!"

"I didn't do it," she said quickly, her voice rising. "I swear, Dániel, I didn't. But Charles... he thinks I did. He confessed to protect me."

Dániel's shoulders sagged, and he pressed a hand to his forehead. "This family," he muttered. "Secrets, lies... it's all tangled."

"That's why we need answers," I said firmly. "About you, about Evelyn's connection to you. Beatrice discovered something before she died. Something about your relationship with Evelyn's mother. I need to know the truth."

Dániel hesitated, glancing at Evelyn, who looked away, her arms wrapped tightly around herself. He took a deep breath. "Evelyn's mother and I were close," he admitted, his voice quiet but steady. "Too close for me to be with a married woman. She told me to stay away after Evelyn was born. She said it would make things easier, but I..." His voice faltered. "I never stopped caring."

"Is that why you sent the gifts?" I asked. "The dolls, the letters?"

"Yes," he said, his gaze dropping. "I thought... I thought she'd know I cared. Even if I couldn't be there, I wanted her to feel my presence."

"She did," Evelyn said, her voice trembling. "But it wasn't enough. You weren't here."

"I know," Dániel said, his voice thick with regret. "I should have been. I should have fought harder."

The raw emotion in his voice softened something in Evelyn's expression, and for a moment, the tension between them eased. But the questions swirling in my mind refused to settle.

"You're here now," I said. "And we need your help. Beatrice discovered the truth. Did she ever contact you? Confront you?"

"No," Dániel said firmly. "I haven't spoken to anyone in this family for years."

I studied his face, searching for any hint of deception, but all I saw was sorrow. Still, his arrival added another layer to the tangled web of motives and secrets surrounding Beatrice's death.

"This conversation isn't over," I said, straightening. "But it's not one we can have here."

"Why not?" Evelyn asked, frowning.

"Because I know who killed Beatrice," I said, my voice steady. "And it's time we all heard the truth."

**

The snug at The Olde Jolly Hall was thick with tension, the storm outside battering the windows with icy fury. The fire crackled warmly in the hearth, its flickering light casting long shadows that danced across the room. Chairs had been arranged in a semicircle around me, and each person sat rigidly, their faces a mix of wariness, defiance, and barely concealed dread.

Wiggles leaned casually against the doorframe, his sharp eyes scanning the room like a hawk surveying its prey. Despite his relaxed posture, his presence lent the gathering an air of authority. I took a deep breath, the warmth of the room doing little to ease the chill of anticipation that gripped me. This was it—the moment to unravel the tangled threads and expose the truth.

"Thank you all for coming," I began, my voice steady despite the nervous energy coursing through me. "I know the past few days have been overwhelming, but I believe it's time we uncover who killed Beatrice Harper."

The room fell silent, save for the faint howl of the wind

outside. Evelyn sat closest to the fire, her hands clasped tightly in her lap, her pale face illuminated by the glow of the flames. Beside her was Dániel Lukács, his posture stiff and his gaze fixed on his daughter with quiet concern. Charles sat near the window, his jaw tight, his fingers drumming a restless rhythm on the armrest of his chair. Paula's hands were folded primly in her lap, her expression carefully neutral, while Melinda perched on the edge of her seat, her polished demeanour intact but her eyes betraying a flicker of unease. Gilbert, ever the dramatist, was draped in his scarf like a theatrical prop, his teacup balanced delicately in one hand.

I turned my attention to Evelyn first. "Evelyn," I began, meeting her wide eyes, "you had a motive. Beatrice discovered that Dániel was your father and intended to expose the truth, cutting you out of the Harper estate. That would have been devastating, both emotionally and financially."

Evelyn's lips trembled, and she shook her head. "I didn't do it," she said, her voice raw with emotion. "Beatrice hated me, yes, but she was still my sister. I could never hurt her."

I nodded, her sincerity evident in her tone and posture. "I believe you," I said gently. "Your actions that night don't align with the evidence. You were hurt, Evelyn, but you're not a killer."

Relief washed over her face, and Dániel placed a steadying hand on her arm. I shifted my focus to Charles, who straightened slightly, his sharp gaze meeting mine.

"Charles," I said, "you confessed to killing Beatrice. You said you argued in the passageway, that you pushed her and panicked. But the injuries she sustained don't match that story."

He bristled, his shoulders squaring. "I was trying to

protect Evelyn," he said gruffly. "If taking the blame kept her safe, I was willing to do it."

"You shouldn't have, Charles!" Evelyn exclaimed. She jumped from her chair and threw herself at her older brother, pummelling his chest with her fists before collapsing in tears. Charles draped his arms around her and planted a soft kiss on the top of her head.

"Your confession was an act of love, not guilt," I replied. "But Beatrice wasn't pushed. She was struck with a heavy object. Someone else killed her."

Charles' jaw tightened, and he looked away, guilt and frustration warring in his expression. I moved on to Paula, who stiffened when she met my gaze.

"Paula," I said, "your access to the Hall's finances put you in a precarious position. If Beatrice had discovered any discrepancies, you would have had a reason to silence her."

Her eyes flashed with indignation. "I've worked for this family for years," she said firmly. "I handled the books with care, but I never took anything that didn't belong to me. Beatrice was thorough—if she'd found something, she would have confronted me directly. I had no reason to kill her."

I studied her for a moment, then gave a slight nod. "Your loyalty to the Hall is evident, Paula. I don't believe you're involved."

Her posture relaxed slightly, though the tension in the room remained palpable. I turned to Dániel, whose expression was guarded but intense.

"Dániel," I said, "there's a photo of you with Beatrice. You claim you haven't seen her since she was a child, yet this photo suggests otherwise. Can you explain it?"

He frowned, confusion creasing his brow. "I haven't seen

Beatrice in years," he said, his tone adamant. "That's the truth."

I held the image up for him to see, watching his reaction closely. His expression shifted from confusion to realisation. "That's... that's not me. Look, their hair is dark. Mine's been grey for at least two years. Someone must have impersonated me," he said slowly. "That's the only explanation."

My pulse quickened as the puzzle pieces clicked into place. Like many people, Dániel had an online presence, but the photos of him on the internet were carefully hand chosen and not updated as he aged. Beatrice had done her research, but the first rule of our image conscious world had tripped her up. Dániel had gone grey.

I turned to Melinda, who sat perfectly still, her composure unnervingly intact.

"Melinda," I said, my voice steady, "you had access to Beatrice's communications—emails, schedules, personal documents. You knew about the photo, didn't you? You arranged the meeting."

Her lips parted slightly, but no words came. The silence was damning.

"Someone has been communicating as Beatrice after her death. Nobody has unrivalled access to her accounts like you do," I continued, stepping closer.

"Beatrice was like a sister to me. Of course she trusted me with everything."

"She discovered the financial discrepancies in the Hall's accounts and she confronted you."

"It wasn't stealing. It was taking payment that was rightly mine for the hours nobody saw."

To my surprise, Paula huffed at that. "You think you're the only member of staff here who works hard? I could give you a dozen or more names of people who are starting early and finishing late. They don't put their hands in the till!"

"You killed her because she discovered what you'd been doing."

Melinda's calm façade cracked. Her hands clenched the edge of her chair, and her eyes darted around the room. "I didn't mean to," she whispered, her voice trembling. "She wouldn't listen. She said she'd ruin me, that she'd destroy everything I'd worked for. I panicked."

"You struck her," I said, my voice firm. "To protect yourself."

"No!" Melinda shrieked. "To protect the two of us."

"The two of who?" I asked.

Melinda gazed across at Charles, his arms still wrapped around Evelyn. "We're in love."

"Melinda," Charles' voice was a warning.

Melinda's composed face began to crumble, as if made from quick sand. "We're getting married. You said, Charles. You said if only Beatrice wasn't in the way, we could be together. We could run the Hall."

Charles swallowed. "I said a lot of things. You really can't run away with these ideas. It could never last, you know that. I mean," he scoffed, "you're staff."

Melinda roared in anger, reached for a candelabra on a small table beside her, and moved swiftly across the room in Charles' direction.

"Charles!" I shouted, but his position was too awkward, his sister was draped around him, and Melinda was moving so quickly. She was barely a few steps from him when she clattered to the floor.

Gilbert, standing by the wall with one foot out, gasped. "Goodness, did I trip you? I can be such a clumsy elf!"

Wiggles stepped forward, his handcuffs gleaming in the firelight.

"Melinda North," he said formally, "you're under arrest for the murder of Beatrice Harper."

As Wiggles secured the cuffs, Melinda looked around the room, her gaze lingering on each of us. "I just wanted to matter," she said, her voice breaking. "You don't understand what it's like to give everything you have and still be invisible."

The storm outside seemed to ease as Melinda was led away, her footsteps echoing through the snug. Evelyn buried her face in her hands, while Dániel placed a protective arm around her shoulders. Charles stared at the fire, his expression a mix of guilt and relief. Paula let out a shaky breath, and Gilbert, ever dramatic, took a bow for his part in apprehending her.

As the door closed behind Wiggles and Melinda, the room fell into a heavy silence. The truth had been laid bare, but its weight lingered, leaving the Harper family fractured but free from deception.

It was Paula who broke the silence. "The Hall's been through worse," she said, her voice steely firm. "We'll weather this storm, just like we always have. And with Beatrice gone... we'll be looking to the two of you for our orders now."

Charles and Evelyn looked at her, then, as if synchronised, they each gave a defiant nod.

14

The grand hall of The Olde Jolly Hall had been transformed into a winter wonderland. Snowflake-shaped fairy lights twinkled overhead, casting a soft glow over garlands of holly and ivy draped along the wooden beams. A towering Christmas tree stood near the altar, its branches heavy with glittering ornaments and topped with a golden star that seemed to wink at the gathered crowd. The air was rich with the scent of pine, spiced cider, and freshly baked gingerbread, creating an atmosphere so cozy it felt like stepping into a Christmas dream.

I stood just outside the grand oak doors, my hands clasped tightly around my bouquet of winter roses and sprigs of mistletoe. My wedding dress shimmered in the candlelight, the delicate snowflake embroidery on the bodice catching every flicker of light. Mrs Claus bustled around me, fluffing my veil and adjusting the small, intricate brooch pinned just above my heart.

"Darling, you look divine," Mrs Claus said, stepping

back to admire her handiwork. "Nick's heart will stop when he sees you."

I smiled, though my heart fluttered nervously. "Do you think everything's perfect? The decorations, the music?"

Mrs Claus' eyes sparkled. "It's magical, my dear. Exactly as it should be. But remember, it's not the flowers or the lights that make this day special. It's the love you and Nick share. Now, no more fretting. It's time."

Just then, the door burst open and Einstein galloped in, his eyes wide in panic.

"Whoa, what's wrong buddy?" I asked the young reindeer.

"We've got a bow-tie emergency! Mine won't stay straight, and Betty's insisting she needs perfume to 'set the tone' for the wedding!"

The leisurely clops of Betty's elegant sauntering followed behind. "August gave me a little spritz, but I'm a larger lady and very proud of it. I'll need more Chan... oh!"

I flushed as I realised the sight of me in my dress had brought Betty to a complete standstill, physically and verbally.

"You look like a princess," Betty said once she had recovered. She raised a hoof and I allowed her to stroke the luxurious fabric of the gown. Betty had better hygiene standards than many humans I knew, and sure enough the dress remained spotless after she had let go.

"Thank you, Betty. Now, Einstein, find Gilbert. He's a master when it comes to bow ties."

"Yes, ma'am!" Einstein said, raising his own hoof to salute me before scampering out of the room.

"And for my own predicament?" Betty asked.

I laughed and reached into the small bag I had brought

with me. Inside was a lipstick in a soft pink shade, a compact mirror that I had had since childhood, and many packs of tissues. There was no chance of my surviving the day without crying.

"Here, take this," I said. I handed Betty the Chanel No5 that August had bought me as a wedding gift. It had been a sweet idea, but the expensive perfume seemed too grown up for me somehow. Betty would have no such qualms about the unopened bottle.

She squealed with excitement. A strange noise coming from a reindeer who appeared to be wearing many coats of mascara. "You are a life saver!"

I laughed, and she gave me a wink before leaving the room.

Juts a few moments later, the doors creaked open, revealing a path lined with candlelit lanterns leading to the altar. The gathered guests turned in their seats, and a collective sigh of admiration swept through the room. At the end of the aisle, Nick stood tall and dashing in his winter-themed suit, his expression a mixture of awe and joy as his eyes locked onto me.

"Ready, my dear?" a deep, warm voice asked.

I turned to find Father Christmas standing beside her, his red velvet suit trimmed with gold embroidery that sparkled in the soft light. His kind eyes twinkled, and his gloved hand extended toward me.

"I'm ready," she said, slipping her hand into his.

The room seemed to hold its breath as Father Christmas escorted me down the aisle. The gentle jingle of his sleigh bells, attached discreetly to his boots, added a festive melody to the moment, perfectly in tune with the magic of the day. Guests wiped tears from their eyes, and even Gilbert, standing near the altar, dabbed dramatically at his with a lace handkerchief. Mrs Claus beamed proudly from the front row, a glimmer of tears sparkling in her eyes as she leaned into August, who had managed to cry so much her mascara had run and left her looking like a panda. Tom gave me an apologetic smile and gestured to his arms, where he rocked a fast asleep and utterly unimpressed baby Jeb. Einstein, the excitable young reindeer, craned his neck to get a better view, his antlers adorned with tiny twinkling lights, while Betty, perched next to him with a spritz of her signature perfume lingering in the air, offered a knowing smile that seemed to say, "About time, Holly."

Paula sat with a quiet dignity, her usual reserve softened by the warmth of the moment, while Charles, looking unusually serene, held Evelyn's hand as a rare show of solidarity between the siblings. In the row behind them, Wiggles, the ever-professional Chief Inspector, sat tall and proud at the back of the room, his stoic expression betraying the faintest hint of a smile as he observed the joyful gathering. Mitzy sat beside him, but was too busy scrawling notes on her clipboard to watch my entrance. That elf was never off duty!

I grinned as I saw Nadine and Marcie from the book club, their handbags suspiciously bulging. I knew they'd each got at least one book stuffed in there, to get through any lulls in the festivities.

The snug room, now transformed with garlands of holly and twinkling fairy lights, seemed to wrap everyone in a warm embrace. The faint scent of cinnamon and pine filled the air, mingling with the occasional burst of giggles from the children as they whispered about the "real" Santa Claus. It was a gathering of friends, family, and unexpected allies, all united in this magical moment as the cozy, festive spirit of Candy Cane Hollow enveloped us all.

When we reached Nick, standing at the altar beside his *best wo-man* Ginger, Father Christmas placed my hand in his with a smile. "Take care of her," he said softly, his voice full of warmth and authority.

Nick nodded, his eyes never leaving mine. "Yes, Dad. Always."

"I'll kill him if he doesn't," Ginger said with a wink that didn't make her threat any less terrifying.

Gilbert, resplendent in his role as officiant, cleared his throat and stepped forward. "Ladies, gentlemen, and magical creatures of Candy Cane Hollow," he began, his voice grand and theatrical, "we are gathered here today to witness the union of Holly and Nick, two souls as perfectly matched as cinnamon and sugar, as marshmallows and cocoa."

A ripple of laughter spread through the crowd, lightening the emotional charge of the moment. Betty and Einstein, two of our reindeer, stood near the front, dressed in festive collars. Einstein whispered something to Betty, who nodded enthusiastically. I could smell the Chanel perfume from where I stood - she must have bathed in it.

Gilbert continued, blending his usual flair with heartfelt sincerity. He spoke of love and partnership, of the courage it takes to solve mysteries—and sometimes, to solve the puzzle of another's heart. Finally, he turned to the two of us.

"Nick, do you promise to stand by Holly's side through sleigh chases and snowstorms, to support her in all her adventures, and to never, ever eat the last gingerbread man without asking?"

Nick grinned. "I do."

"And Holly," Gilbert said, turning to me, "do you promise to cherish Nick through mysteries and mischief, to laugh with him, and to keep the Christmas spirit alive in your hearts, no matter the season?"

My smile softened, and my voice was steady. "I do."

As we exchanged rings, the warmth in the room seemed to grow, enveloping everyone present. The love between us was palpable, a beacon that shone brighter than the storm outside. Gilbert's voice rang out with triumph.

"By the powers vested in me by the good people of Candy Cane Hollow, I now pronounce you husband and wife. You may kiss the bride!"

Nick cupped my face gently, our kiss sealing the vows as the room erupted into cheers and applause. The reindeer stomped their hooves in approval, and Mrs Claus dabbed at her eyes with a snowy-white handkerchief embroidered with holly leaves.

The reception that followed was a feast of cozy delights. Tables were laden with steaming mugs of cocoa, mulled wine, and an array of festive treats. The centrepiece was a towering gingerbread house adorned with intricate icing designs, a testament to Gilbert's baking prowess.

As the newlyweds - us! - danced to a soft, lilting tune, I looked around the room, my heart full. Evelyn and Dániel were talking quietly in a corner, their smiles tentative but genuine. Paula and Wiggles were deep in conversation, their heads close together. Even Melinda's absence—though bittersweet—felt like the close of a necessary chapter.

Nick leaned in, his breath warm against her ear. "What are you thinking about, Mrs Wood?"

I laughed softly, leaning my head against his shoulder. "Just how perfect this moment is. And how lucky I am."

He pulled me closer, his strong arms a steady anchor. "I'm the lucky one."

The storm outside had finally quieted, the snow falling

gently now, blanketing the world in a soft glow. Inside, the warmth of love and laughter filled every corner of The Olde Jolly Hall, carrying Nick and I into the start of our happily ever after.

THE END

PRE-ORDER THE NEXT BOOK NOW: NUTCRACKER CONSPIRACY

ABOUT THE AUTHOR

Mona Marple is a lover of all things book-related. When she isn't working on her next release, she's probably curled up somewhere warm reading a good story.

Mona is a fan of all things festive and is looking forward to adding to the Christmas Cozy Mystery series over the years. Her other cozy mysteries include the Waterfell Tweed series, the Mystic Springs paranormal series and the Mexican Mysteries series.

Mona lives in Nottinghamshire, England with her bread baking husband, her always-singing daughter, and their pampered Labradoodle, Coco. In fact, Mona's online reader group were a big part of persuading Mona's husband to welcome Coco into their home!

Stay up to date with her latest news by joining her eMail list at http://www.monamarple.com/vip-readers

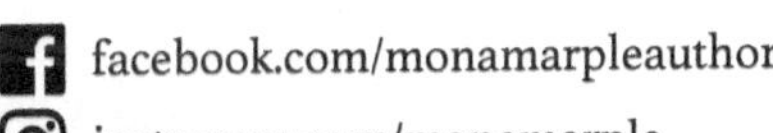

facebook.com/monamarpleauthor

instagram.com/monamarple